Under A Hunter Moon

Cauldron Falls-Sylvan Valley Founding Families, Volume 2

Solara Gordon

Published by THE EARTH MOVED, LLC, 2026.

This is a work of fiction. Similarities to real people, places, or events are entirely coincidental.

UNDER A HUNTER MOON

First edition. March 2, 2026.

ISBN: 979-8995183617

Written by Solara Gordon.

Also by Solara Gordon

Cascade Bay

Love Reborn

Reunited By Choice

Love's Triple Play

Three Hearts In Love

For the Love of Three

Cauldron Falls

Believe In Love

Home for the Holidays

Three Hearts Entwined

A Mate of Their Own

Moonlit Match

A Christmas Reunion

Cauldron Falls-Sylvan Valley Founding Families

Blue Moon Valentine

Under A Hunter Moon

Peyton Corners

Falling for You

Caught by Love's Slow Burn

Sylvan Valley

No Other Magic Necessary

Claimed by the Wolf

Standalone

A Heart's Desire

To Love You Again

To Love You Again

Watch for more at https://solaragordon.com/.

Dedication

Inspiration comes from many places. Chase, Kim and Slade's story inspiring members of Solara's Glamourous Stars are: Kim Kurtz, LaGina Keisha Hagerman-Reese, Christine Heydt, Joy Compton Boutwell, and Brenda Chambers. Thank you for choosing characters names, traits and setting. You inspired a polyamorous why choose theme second chance paranormal fantasy romance. Writing Chase, Kim and Slade's story bloomed and flowed due to your input.

A special thank you goes to Chevy Allen, my beta reader. You read bits and pieces, commented and shared input from a reader standpoint and view. This greatly helped enrich and add depth to Chase, Kim and Slade.

LaGina and Christine, your older polyamorous matchmakers' story is in the offing. Let's see what two older why choose matchmaking magics have to say when their second chance at romance happens.

This one is for my readers. The ones that inspire me and share their story ideas.

Smiles,

Solara Gordon

CHAPTER ONE

"I'm not choosing one." Kim Cortez faced her Aunt LaGina Gibson. "I chose one last time. Everything fell apart. Left at the altar. Embarrassed and—"

"Kim, lower your voice." LaGina Gibson glanced over her shoulder. "Several tables are watching us."

Kim slumped in her seat, heaving an exasperated sigh. "Look, just because I own Owens doesn't mean I have to fake smile every time I work."

"No, you don't." LaGina leaned forward, continuing to speak in a whispered tone. "Not ranting and raving about your personal life is better than all Cauldron Falls' gossips knowing."

Kim nodded. "Yeah, Zach swears his subscriptions doubled with the Wednesday Tell It All section."

LaGina chuckled. "The around-town announcements and events section. Zach hired Christine Flowers to edit that section and the children's page."

"I'm going to burst the eavesdropping gossips present." Kim stood. "I think the two new wines from Sylvan Valley Vineyards are a good choice."

LaGina smiled as she stood. "I'll let Slade know. He's supposed to be back from a vintner's conference this weekend."

Kim pressed her lips together, curling them in her best non-fake smile. "Good. I'll reach out to his manager, Chase, beginning of the week."

LaGina looked away. Raising Kim hadn't been easy. Getting her to understand that her mixed shifter heritage wouldn't allow her to morph into any animal. Having multiple animal totems and spirit guides drove her nightmares and dreams until Christine had taught her dream magic. The elusive escape magic that permitted one to talk with their guides and totems in a common language. LaGina hoped Christine and her attorney had looked over the business contract for Matchups Elite.

Matchmaking older magicals, supernaturals and shapeshifters had grown more than LaGina anticipated. Their first Sadie Hawkins event could be as early as next month's first full moon. Late summer and fall harvest full moons brought people in. The closer to the holidays people got, the fuller Sadie Hawkins events got.

LaGina slung her purse over her shoulder, picked up her tote brief, and faced Kim. "Call me later tonight. I've got a meeting with clients until closing time."

"Thank you, Aunt LaGina." Kim hugged her aunt and walked her to Owen's front door. "I made a huge mistake trying to choose one before. That's not who I am."

LaGina cupped Kim's cheek. "Darlin', you gotta be you. Be who you are. There's always going to be ones that disapprove. Don't let that stop you from finding happiness and the love that awaits you."

"Aunt LaGina, love that awaits me?" Kim folded her arms tight across her chest, glaring at her aunt. "You been lighting too many matchmaker candles again?"

LaGina smiled and lowered her hand. "No, everyone has their time. I'm wishing you have yours now. This year."

Kim shook her head, hugged her aunt again and stepped back. "Keep wishing. Keep lighting the candles. Tell Christine I said hello and to work her crystal magic on those tarot cards you swear are telling you I'm finding the love of my life soon."

LaGina rolled her eyes and exited Owens.

Kim flexed her hands and shrugged. She loved her aunt. Her second mom became her first after her parents' untimely passing. Kim rubbed her hands together. Her accountant's voice mail had caught her off guard. Owen's first-quarter revenue was more than predicted. More than enough to pay every bill in full and a down payment on expanding Owen's to Sylvan Valley and possibly Nashville and Chattanooga. Wine and ice cream drinks, fast food specialties and once a month, all you could eat barbecue buffet fit right in with Cauldron Falls foodies, Sylvan Valley's wine snobs, and the upcoming Millennials from both towns and moving to their area.

Goddess help her to understand why small towns. More magical and shapeshifter hybrids plus limited magic mortals flocked to the area. Cauldron Falls and Sylvan Valley were no longer unknown small towns oasis for magicals, shapeshifters and supernaturals looking for a place below the national radar.

Kim started down the short hall leading to her office. The door with the large sign that read storage authorized personnel only. She laughed as she reached for the doorknob. On the other side was her private getaway zone. The one place she decorated without anyone's suggestions or input. She gripped the doorknob, jerked her hand back and stared at the door. The hair on the back of her neck ruffled again. It was like static electricity rushed over and through her. The pit of her stomach flip-flopped twice. She'd eaten breakfast and gulped two cups of black tea before lunch. Was the lunch special tainted? Great, now a food poisoning situation. She needed more problems like an iceberg wanted sunshine reflecting onto it from overly warm waters.

The doorknob slowly turned. Kim stepped back. She pivoted, ready to bolt down the hall, screaming out '*everyone evacuate*'. Magic gone awry wasn't worth combating if the person casting it was on the other side. Teleportation was one of the forbidden magics for a damn good reason. Most couldn't control the spell or the concept.

The door opened wider. Kim stumbled backwards, trying to tear her gaze away from the entity standing in the doorway. "How? You?"

Slade Stoneworth wished he hadn't agreed to meet with Owen's new head chef, Adam Drake. Adam insisted they meet at Owen's to sample proposed food and wine combinations. Blast it, Adam's job required his connoisseur palate be on duty and the expert on tweaking tastes. A triple smashed burger with a touch of hot sauce, shredded Colby Jack and Munster cheese mix plus marinated mushrooms on a lightly toasted brioche bun slathered with garlic aoli mayo suited his stomach and taste buds just fine. Adam had promised such an exquisite, tasty item fifteen minutes ago. Fresh-made patties didn't take that long to cook. Homemade kettle chips were already waiting for garlic salt and pepper. Slade smelled them the moment he entered through the kitchen service entry. Granted he'd dozed off shortly after Adam exited the studio-sized office complete with a pull-out sofa bed couch. Why had Adam left him in here awaiting the promised culinary delight?

Footsteps. He heard footsteps. Finally, Adam was back with his lunch. Rate time was going, probably an early dinner. Chase awaited him back at the vineyard. The bookkeeper threatened to raise her rates if they didn't organize their system better. Too many papers and not enough automation. Had Chase put his undergrad accounting minor to work? Created an easy entry system for both sales and tracking the aging process? The vineyard was ready to double sales. Exporting outside of Sylvan Valley and Cauldron Falls. In-state sales were starting thanks to advertising.

Slade reached for the doorknob. He inhaled again. That wasn't food he smelled. It was—no, it couldn't be. The last time he smelled that pheromone and hormone mix was ten years ago. A night of sultry passion. Shared pleasure and he'd found out Chase had won. Except he hadn't. Another guy named Terrence. From a Chicago pack yanked the pheromones and hormones owner away from them. What was Adam doing? Adam knew better than trying to reignite a former matchmake that fizzled out.

Kim took a step forward. She blinked twice, squinted, and slowly exhaled. Slade Stoneworth. All six-foot-three of him filled her office doorway. Who had let him in?

"Excuse me, Kim. Coming through."

Kim turned. Adam approached pushing a cart with a covered tray on top. An ice bucket with what appeared to be three soda cans in it and glasses next to it. She stuck her hand out. Adam slowed.

"You better have a good explanation." Kim nodded toward Slade. "Damn good reason why he's here."

Adam stopped close to her. "I invited Slade here to discuss the wines we're interested in purchasing. Plus let him sample some of our haute cuisine. Lunch meeting. Didn't expect you in today."

"You don't check the posted schedule?" Kim pointed at the soda cans. "Who else did you invite?"

Adam grinned. "Well, since Enrique told me you were here—you know. . ."

Kim rolled her eyes as she spoke. "You decided a three-way business luncheon was a grand idea."

"Actually killing two items with one stone. Slade and I discussing the wines and what dishes they are used for or in. You and he pricing the purchase and me knowing what I got to work with creating new ice creams and meal entrées." Adam pushed the cart forward. "I'd like to eat before it gets cold."

Kim moved aside, motioning Adam forward. Slade knew she was here. No way to deny that. They'd seen each other. Her aunt's visit had come as she wanted to take an early break and walk through town checking out the businesses up and down their street. Kim sniffed. Her stomach gurgled. The odors rolling off the cart as Adam passed teased her palate. Did Triple Mashed Burgers with the works await them? Her stomach growled. Kim looked down and back up. Adam and Slade stood in the doorway watching her. She strode forward. Her psyche could stop flashing past passionate moments with Slade and one other person. Thank Deities, the other person wasn't Adam.

"Hey Slade, sorry I'm late." Adam pushed the serving card into the office. "Had to thaw the ground bison."

"Bison?" Slade reached for the ice bucket rattling close to the edge of the cart.

"Yeah, premium stuff. That's why this is called Tastebud Savory. Figured new items to go with premium wines. Good combinations attract more sales." Adam pushed the cart next to Kim's desk.

Slade set the ice bucket and sodas on the desk. "I see we have a third person joining us."

Kim waved as she passed Adam. She made her way around the desk and sat in her desk chair. "Greetings Slade. Nice you could join Adam and me for lunch."

Adam glanced from Kim to Slade and back. Lupa on high, he planned this meeting figuring Slade and Kim could talk pricing and ordering at the same time. Why did he get the feeling there were a couple of hotheads waiting to explode? Nothing he could do about it now. Once Slade and Kim's hangries were lulled and pacified, he could poke the meeting into a confab win for Sylvan Valley Winery and Owens. Adam swore miscellaneous duties didn't include referee, bookkeeper, and influencer. If his did, he needed one big raise.

"Let's eat before it gets cold." Adam lifted the lid off the covered platter, waving his hand, hoping the smells kindled taste buds clamoring for satisfaction instead of scowls and sideways glances.

"Did you bring some of your homemade kettle chips?" Kim asked, reaching for the burger closest to her.

Adam uncovered the bowl he set next to the platter. "Sure, did. Lightly salted, a bit of garlic, and pepper mixed with a squeeze of ghost pepper juice. Tangy with a kick."

Slade sat in the chair close to where Adam stood. Adam put a plate in front of Slade, put a handful of chips on the plate plus the burger closest to him. Slade nodded and spread his napkin across his lap. Adam passed a plate with chips on it to Kim. *Deities, please let them eat in peace and not pieces of peace.* His lunch break had come and gone training the relief cook and new dishwasher on how things worked and the way he ran his kitchen.

Slade held up his hand. "May we eat and enjoy in peace. Discuss why we're all here once the food begins to settle?"

Adam nodded as he sat. Slade glanced at Kim. She nodded and shrugged. Great talk about a double-edged meaning. That hadn't changed.

Twenty minutes later, Adam placed the empty platter, plates, bowl, and ice bucket on the servicing cart. He wiped his mouth and tossed his napkin on the cart. "Anyone want another soda?"

Kim drummed her fingers on the desk. "You think it's safe to leave Slade and me alone?"

Adam slumped lower in his chair. What the hell had he walked into without knowing what ingredients he tossed together?

"Look, I don't know what you're talking about. I tried to check two things off the to-do list you and I discussed last week. New wines, new dishes, and a new menu spotlighting them. We talked about supporting local businesses. Wine and Sylvan Valley Winery are well known. I figured this was a good meeting set up." Adam poured the rest of his soda into his glass and crushed the can with his hand.

Slade didn't bother to hide his mirth. He chuckled and leaned forward, pointing to Kim. "I'm here on business. Winery business. I can cut you a deal on prices, delivery and keep you stocked with some of the best wine in the tri-county area."

Kim slid a legal pad partway across the desk. She shoved it the remainder of the way to Slade as she spoke. "Can you interpret recipes? Understand the finer nuances of cooking? Or ice cream making? Alcohol content and level need to be almost zero on cooking wines or ice cream ones. Then there's the drinking stuff."

Slade pushed the pad aside. He rose, walked around the desk, and leaned forward, placing his hands on the desk close to Kim. He whispered as he spoke. "Unless you want to spill the beans to your chef, I suggest we keep past personal out of this. I'll ink in a slot to discuss how hot I can get you for another day and time if you're that much in need. I still remember the places you like nipped while Chase licked and sucked your clitoris."

Kim scooted her chair back, creating space between her and Slade. "Slade, that price of seven dollars and fifty cents per gallon for cooking wine sounds like what Adam and I are looking for."

Slade grinned, winked the eye Adam could not see and made his way back to his seat. Oh, getting Kim hot and bothered had its merits. Merits that only he, Chase and Kim needed to know about. He wondered if Chase was up to luring Kim back into their arms.

"We haven't tasted the wine yet." Adam stood. "I thought we'd arrange a visit to do that. Talk about what wines might work with the recipes and ideas that's on the pad."

Slade perched on the edge of the desk. He picked up the pad, ran his finger up and down the page, flipped the sheet and traced the next page line by line with his finger. He tossed the pad on the desk. "Cooking wines are the first draw from the barrels as they reach initial fermentation. I can supply what you need for that easily."

Kim slapped her weekly planner on the desk. "Okay. That takes care of the entrée needs. What about the ice cream?"

"You need to taste. Sip and savor before you decide what wines will come close to that level. *Excellent repeat request is what you are aiming for, right?*" Slade reached for the weekly planner. Kim put her hand on it.

"Perhaps you need to talk with your vineyard manager before you commit to anything else." Kim picked up the pencil she'd tossed on the desk. "Penciling things in lets for changes that inking in doesn't. No need to ghost a meeting."

"There's phone calendars. A lot more efficient and conservation-friendly." Slade scrolled through the calendar on his phone. He nodded as he came to a date. He laid the phone on the desk, turned it to Kim and said, "Next Tuesday. Three PM. Chase will meet you at the tasting room to finalize the samples. Chase will arrange a meeting with Adam after that."

Kim pulled the phone to her. She flipped the planner to that date, scribbled in the time and place. She pushed the phone back to Slade careful to not touch him. The burst of energy from Slade's lingering fingerprint DNA reached out inching toward her. Calling out to her inner totem matrix. She wasn't falling again. Caution and awareness had to happen this time. "You're still penciled in. I'll add to my phone calendar. I suspect you best check with Chase. I hope you remember how much he hates being caught off-guard."

"People do change." Slade picked up his phone, saluted Adam, and walked to the office door.

Slade turned and walked back to Adam holding out his hand.

Adam stood and stared at Slade's hand. "What's that for?"

Slade chuckled. "Old-fashioned manners. Congratulations on an awesome lunch. Short business meeting and send me an email with those recipes. I think Sylvan Valley Vineyard and Owens are about to ink a deal that has far-reaching capabilities."

Adam shook Slade's hand, glanced at Kim who shrugged and let go of Slade's hand.

Slade quickly made his way around the desk, almost trapping Kim against the back wall. He placed both palms on the wall, blocking her exit. "This, my dearest, is a reminder of what you missed out on. Missed out on a lot."

Slade lowered his head, bared his teeth, and worried Kim's earlobe. Kim rocked sideways. Slade copied her move. He let go of Kim's earlobe, pulled back some, and brushed his lips over hers as he lowered his hands. His fingers traced circles around her taut nipples. He'd marked her again. Perhaps this time, she would realize there was no easy escape. Especially with a business agreement in place and reputations at stake.

CHAPTER TWO

Kim got up, walked to her office door, and swung it shut. The thud echoed through the office. She was sure Slade heard it and probably felt it as he sauntered down the hall thinking he'd one-upped her again. If he thought he and Chase could top her like previously, they had another thing coming. None of them were kinky or leather groupies. She'd learned a thing about being dominant. Being assertive and damn well not letting either of them think they called the shots alone or gang up on her. Friends in the right places and dominants that understood her need to assert herself without being aggressive unless needed taught her the signs. The signals and the thoughts that could send her pheromones and hormones scampering toward the ones that needed controlling.

Adam dusted his hands on his chef's jacket and grabbed the servicing cart. He started toward the office door. “Glad you enjoyed the lunch and got the meeting set up. Thanks.”

“Sit down, Adam.” Kim made her way back to her desk.

Adam halted, let go of the cart and quickly sat down. “Uh, what's up?”

Adam ducked his head. Lupa, she'd done it without thinking. Trumped Adam into thinking she was upset. Kim came around her desk and sat in the chair next to Adam. She laid her hand on his arm.

“I'm sorry if I came across upset." Kim hesitated, hoping Adam looked up. She never thought him to be submissive. He went toe toe-to-toe with her more than once about Owens' menu and hiring staff.

Adam's gaze met hers. Kim nodded and continued speaking. "You did great. You took the initiative like we discussed. You're head chef and you get a say in what Owens offers. I know that we didn't unite as we'd planned. I didn't know Slade would be here. I planned on calling Chase, his vineyard manager, next week and set up a teleconference."

"Do business from afar?" Adam leaned back in the chair.

"Yeah, hem and haw. Make them negotiate. Instead, Slade tried to pull a bluff. No poker face slick, trying to outfox his client." Kim slid her hand off Adam's arm. "I'll share this. Chase, Slade, and I know each other. Done business before. That's all I'm gonna say."

Adam shook his head. "If it doesn't pertain to getting the wines we need and the negotiations, I don't need to know. I'm your head chef. Not a business partner."

Kim nodded and stood. She picked up the pad off the desk and handed it to Adam. "Go ahead and have Marguerite transcribe these, please. She'll love the side work since she's done with the bookkeeping for the month."

Adam clasped the pad. "Hiring my wife keeps her out of trouble. Not so great for me. I gotta behave all the time she's here."

"You think she's here daily?" Kim smirked. "Ask her about Dwayne, her boyfriend. I think you know that your open relationship allows extras on both sides. You need to take time to find your extra. You know, days off?"

Adam grinned as he reached the office door. "There's a couple of ladies I met at the last polyamory meet-up. Belinda and Suzanne. Maybe I could find time for each of them. No double dating. Would wear me out."

Kim laughed and patted Adam's shoulder. "You do need to keep up your strength for work. I might have to give you back-to-back days off."

"Come on, boss lady." Adam turned, facing her more. "Between Marguerite, Belinda and Suzanne, I'd have to come to work to get some peace and quiet after the three of them all in two days."

Kim nodded vigorously. "Yup. I'm up on how to make sure my staff gets to work on time and well rested."

"*Well rested*? *HA!*" Adam pointed at Kim, adding, "Maybe three days a week off would be better."

"You open to ten-hour shifts four days straight?" Kim leaned closer to Adam and whispered, "I think six-hour shifts work better for you. Gives you time to rest up on the drive home."

Adam grinned more as he shook his head. "True, take a short nap before the drive. Traffic can be a snafu at rush hour."

"Speaking of traffic sanfus, isn't it time you head home? Take Marguerite the recipes and grab a bouquet of flowers out of the table vase cooler. More are coming in tomorrow." Kim glanced at her watch. "Larry, Cameron, and Alice can handle the dinner rush. The new servers are done with training. Larry scheduled them for tonight's dinner hours."

"Thanks Kim." Adam grabbed the serving cart handle and dragged it behind him out the office door.

Kim closed the door, leaned against it, and looked around the office. It had been her home for the last four months. Tonight, it was an office once again. Her house was ready. Her furniture moved in and placed. Boxes needed unpacking beyond the quick sheets on the bed. Towels in the bathroom and the kitchen stuff put away. Her clothes hung in her closet. Aunt LaGina had brought Essie and Zeno plus Herman over before she stopped by.

Kim yawned and stretched. Tonight was the night. She'd sleep deeper than she had since coming back to Cauldron Falls. With Essie and Zeno curled up beside her purring contentedly and Herman sprawled in his bed on top of the shoe bench at the foot of the bed warming her feet, tonight's sleep would be deep and blissful. Especially if Slade and Chase stayed out of her dreams. Her psyche could go dream itself into a snore-filled sleep instead of conjuring up images and flashes from the past to taunt her as she slept.

Slade tossed his car keys on his desk. Chase straightened and turned from where he stood. Corner of the room. The corner where all the fermentation room thermostats were. Next to them were the clipboards with calendars, dates and line progression graphs charting each wine. On the desk close to the fireplace center of the old farmhouse's living room back wall held the computer that linked to every other workstation throughout Sylvan Valley Winery's workstations. Printouts littered Chase's desk.

Slade pulled out his desk chair and sank into it. "Before I tell you about my afternoon, what's the latest reports?"

"New thermostats are working. The oak barrels arrived. Tomas and I sampled the red zinfandel we started aging last month. The pear, apple and rose additions are excellent enhancers. Menage a Duo, circa 2025, is aging nicely. Triadic Pleasure is still awaiting its second pressing. The crystalized raw sugar and cinnamon cubes added enough tartness to offset the citrus sweetness. It will be ready come fall, I hope."

"Have a seat." Slade pushed the desk chair close to him toward Chase. "Sounds like you had a productive meeting and afternoon."

Chase laughed. "If cussing out technology and telling Tomas to speak English when he was cussing out losing the wine paddle in one vat, productive, okay."

Slade sat up. "Did you find the paddle?"

"Oh yeah. And learned a few Spanish curse words along the way. Tomas and I agreed that neither of us wanted to don swim goggles and stained swim shorts to find the blasted paddle. Mess straining nets are awesome accessories." Chase sat down. "From your tone, sounds like you had an unexpected luncheon."

"Let me say one word sums up the luncheon." Slade sighed and drummed his fingers on his desk. "I'll say two instead. Kim Cortez."

"Huh?" Chase arched an eyebrow and gawked at him. "You been lunch time napping again?"

"I wish it were that simple." Slade stood and started pacing toward the fireplace and back to his desk as he continued speaking. "She's real. Very real. Chewed my ass out. Assertively too. Oozed alpha-tinged pheromones and hormones mix. She's back in town."

Chase turned his chair. "Visiting her aunt, I bet."

Slade chuckled and leaned on the corner of the desk. "If it were that simple. It's not. She's back. Very largely back. She bought Owens."

"Bought Owens?" Chase stood. "Weren't we going to do that?"

"Plans change." Slade nodded. "Yeah, change. We needed to expand business. Our own restaurant made sense."

Chase smirked and rose. His turn to pace. Three months ago, he'd started a bartender's mixology class online. That led to his interest in the vineyard and Slade's vintner job offer. Manage the wine production and learn about the finer side of owning a vineyard and restaurant. Now what did they do?

"Chase," Slade began as Chase began his return pace from the front door back to the desk. "Nothing changes except now we have an added bonus."

"Bonus?" Chase paused his pacing.

"Yes," Slade motioned him closer. "We got Kim, Owens and maybe a second chance."

"Second chance? With Kim?" Chase dropped back into his chair.

"Kim's considering our winery for her main supplier. We land the contract. It's a big win considering she's changing up Owens' menu, sweets offerings and maybe—just maybe—we get closure on what the hell sent her running five years ago." Slade stood." Adam Drake is her head chef. You know, the dude that apprenticed with his cousin Peter Drake, MacGruder's five-star chef. West coast phenom."

Chase held up his hands. "You love challenges. Kim was the one that got away. Okay. Are you out to claim revenge?"

Slade's scoff told Chase he'd best change his train of thought. Slade closed the space between them. "Look, Chase. You proposed. Didn't talk to me before you did. We both had a chance with Kim."

Chase swiftly scooted his chair back and rose, knocking it over at the same time. "I proposed because Kim talked about going away to Chicago for college. I figured marrying her might be a way to keep the three of us together."

"Yeah, and she turned you down. Two weeks later, she eloped with Terrence Spencer. The dude from the brindle wolf pack. Something about his prospects was much better than anyone's in Cauldron Falls and Sylvan Valley."

"I hear she left Terrence at the altar." Chase grabbed his jacket off the coat rack near the front door. "I've put in a lot of overtime lately. I'm cashing in on the time off instead of extra pay. I'll be back in a couple days. I need space. We both do."

Slade slowly crossed the living room. He flipped the deadbolt lock. Its echo bounced off the thick silence filling the room. He knew from Chase's earlier voice mail and texts that the vat room and aging barrels were fine. Tomas and his assistant would be in tomorrow afternoon to decant several of the barrels, filling taste-testing bottles. Chase was partially correct. Time off and space were something they both needed. Not because Kim dropped back into their lives. An enigma like before. Different. Unique. And the epitome of stubborn, obstinate, and self-protective they'd all been when they first met each other. How much had life and time changed them? Changed each of them.

Slade slid the double barn doors together, closing off the office portion of the front room. The hundred-year-old farmhouse reminded him of his great-grandfather's paintings. The landscape and temperance of a place where magic, supernatural and exceptional happened. If his lawyer's land trust research proved the speculation the land was part of the original land grant, the mix of founding families divvied up between each other setting up the boundaries of Cauldron Falls and Sylvan Valley, Slade had stumbled upon his family's original homestead. Quite by sheer accident. Fertile land. Hills that could support different growing rates for grapes and possibly hops for their next venture, Caulval Beer. The magical buzz that you'd been waiting to savor.

Making his way into the kitchen, Slade looked around the area he'd managed to decorate and cull out his own space. The one other space he could hole up in, in the farthest area away from the hustle and bustle of the workspace at the front of the house was the loft bedroom with the balcony and staircase that connected to the treehouse like storage area over the large storage garage. The studio apartment set up permitted him escape from his public life. Escape into his art studio. The one place his soul could unleash the angst, fear and ruminating need to conquer the resonating echo his father screamed at him and his mother before he stormed out of their lives. "You're a damn hybrid. A lousy mix of your mother's piss poor genes and my weak ones. I could have done better marrying into another pack."

Slade stripped off his clothes, tossed them in the hamper, and raced into his bathroom. His one solace in moments when his scared, afraid small child whimpers filtered to the top of his adult psyche. A warm shower and a glass of fermented tea while he sketched for a bit. Curling up in bed with his latest book and trying to drift off without seeing the rest of the king-sized bed space as empty and lonely. Perhaps Tomas's abuela was right. He needed a couple familiars. Visiting the local pet rescue might be the best way to find the companions who accepted him and he them. Lost souls uniting in a family unit of their own making and choosing.

Chase didn't look back as he made his way down the path leading to the small cottage between the two aging barrel storage barns. The former owner built the cottage for the farm's prior manager. Memories bounced off the walls from time to time during Samhain. The time when the veil between the living and the next realm thinned and parted. Whispers of laughter and joy pierced the night and faded.

He kept two herbal candles close to the fireplace. He lit them each Samhain, welcoming the spirits' shared memories and letting them know the current resident continued caring for the cottage. Whiffs of lavender and orange blossom filled the house. They permeated the walls giving them a low sunlight glow that illuminated where the veil thinned. Last Samhain, the spirits pushed a gift through the veil tearing it open. The tear sealed quickly.

The folded paper floated to the floor and lay there until Chase carefully picked it up. He pinched himself wincing in pain. He had been asleep. Unfolding the paper, he tried to read the writing. Too tired and almost falling asleep on his feet, he laid the paper on his dresser and got into bed. Several days and many dreams later, Menage a Duo's basic recipe was transformed into the juice fermenting in five of the winery's largest barrels.

Chase unlocked the cottage's front door. Flashes of light rippled across the large rectangular mirror over the fireplace. Faces appeared and faded. Smiles and glances at him came and went. He knew the spirits kept watch over the house. Watched the changes that happened to the farm and its new owner and occupants. Slade shrugged and shook his head each time Chase tried to talk about the gift the powers-that-be bestowed upon them daily. Slade did have the heightened senses and whisker twitching happening. Slade's duality animal rarely appeared. He spoke of the brindled colored wolf as a ghostly apparition that appeared to him every thirteenth full moon. A blood red full moon. Slade's wolf was due for a visit in two weeks.

A low growl and purr emitted from deep in Chase's psyche. "Easy Panthera. I know you smell her. Feel her close by. I do, too."

Two golden eyes appeared in the mirror. They blinked and faded. Chase tossed his jacket on the coat peg rack close to the front door and entered the hallway leading to the kitchen and ensuite living area at the rear of the cottage.

Chase paused as he entered the kitchen. Smells of beef and pork greeted him. The crock pot hodgepodge soup he put on before he left for work was nearly done. Emptying his garden of the last carrots, peas and assorted green beans had triggered his morning meditations.

Focusing on where he was and not what he needed to do created an almost Zen-like etherealness to his energy vibrations. He looked up as he pulled the last carrot from the ground. The morning sun peaked over the apex of the roof illuminating the reddish orange of the carrot. Health and vitality oozed through the air pulsating around him as if to say, *Eat me and be one with me. Consume my brethren vegetables with the meat your leopard needs. Know all is well and you are blessed.*

Chase lifted the lid of the crockpot and inhaled. Cilantro, spicy paprika, and a hint of garlic and onion filled his nostrils. Bits of the tangy barbecue sauce he'd marinated the pork short ribs in leaped out grabbing his attention. He stirred the soup, enjoying the rich, multicolored palette the meat and vegetables displayed. He put the lid back on and turned.

Biscuits hot from the oven, slathered with butter or torn into bite-sized pieces to toss in the soup came to mind. The last can from the month's prior shopping trip into Nashville awaited their baked destiny on the top shelf of the fridge. Making his way toward the fridge, two sets of golden eyes greeted him. Chase smiled and squatted down. "Priscilla. Leoda. Come, my loves. Pets await. Then food."

Two medium-sized black cats worked their way off the lower shelf of the lazy susan pantry. Leoda stretched and emitted a soft mew. Priscilla jumped over Leoda, walked up to Chase, and took a swat at him. Priscilla hissed, sat on her haunches, and swished her tail.

Chase chuckled as Priscilla meowed twice and began rubbing against him. "Ah, Prissy. My beautiful old lady. The chill in the air is signaling the change of seasons. You are another year older. Time for your meds after dinner."

Priscilla flapped him with her tail as she walked away. Chase stretched out a hand toward Leoda. Leoda's feralness never left. He chose the people he trusted. The people that he let near or into the cottage. Running up to people, biting them without breaking the skin and diving under the couch was his regular leave me the frack alone signal to strangers and people he didn't trust. Those he adored got mews, headbutts and requests for pets. Often finding themselves with a lap full of a purring black cat. Leoda hadn't come near him for two weeks after neutering him. Now, Leoda followed him through the house. Even into the bathroom while he showered or sat on the commode.

Dinner time for the three of them was now. Chase retrieved the can of biscuits from the fridge and put them on a baking sheet as the oven warmed. Leoda and Priscilla munched kibble mixed with moist food close to the end of the sink counter combination. Twenty minutes later, Chase finished his second bowl of soup and two more biscuits. He leaned back in his chair, yawned, and stretched. Cleaning up the kitchen was simple and easy. Crock pot in the fridge. Biscuits in a bag and in the fridge. Dishes rinsed and in the dishwasher. As he turned out the lights, Leoda and Priscilla followed him toward the bedroom and the rest the peaceful silence and quiet of the house inviting them to slumber deeply.

CHAPTER THREE

Kim stood outside the farmhouse bearing the sign Sylvan Valley Winery Main Offices. Damn it, why had Adam canceled at the last moment coming with her? Even Marguerite had claimed other client meetings instead of coming along as her and Adam's backup. A week's worth of preparation shot to shit. Delegating work hadn't helped one damn bit. Cramming the notes hadn't produced confidence. She worried more about the little shit neither Adam nor Marguerite bothered to fill her in on. Kim turned around ready to bound down the steps and send Slade and Chase a reschedule text.

"Nice view. Especially when the sun sets." An all too familiar voice said from behind her.

Kim unclenched the strap of her courier bag. "Sunset is a long time off."

"True. I doubt our meeting will last that long." Chase moved up beside her. Just within her peripheral vision. His profile hadn't changed much, her psyche chided. Sideview didn't show much. Chase could be butt-ugly for all she knew.

"Slade is in the office finishing up a video conference call. Our resident chef, Michael, will serve lunch before our meeting starts." Chase turned, facing her.

Kim swallowed twice. Ginger red hair. Her memory's matching beard was gone. Chase, clean-shaven, with a short professional office haircut, watched her. He held out his hand. "Good to see you again, Kim."

Kim swiped her hand on her sleeve. Could she bs her way out of the sweaty damn palms her psyche insisted she have? "Sticky fingers. Adam's new donut recipe for breakfast. Maybe I better wash my hands before I touch anything."

Chase grinned, shrugged and walked toward the farmhouse's front door. "Guess you forgot, I can read your pheromones. It's okay you *don't want to touch at this moment*."

Kim took a bottle of hand sanitizer out of her jacket pocket. Squirted some in her hand and rubbed the liquid around her palm and other hand as best she could while holding the bottle. "As soon as I wash them, maybe your reading will change."

"You want me to touch?" Chase moved toward her.

Kim stepped back and down two of the front steps. "Didn't say that."

"Chase, running after our guests again?" Slade asked, stepping out the front door.

"Kim issues challenges. We've never backed down from them." Chase moved on to the first step, leaning toward Kim. "Her pheromonal pulse says touching is what she's aching for."

Slade burst out laughing. "The look in those eyes says I'll beat the shit out of you if you do."

Chase shrugged and moved back up on the porch. "Ah, well. Can't fault me for trying."

Slade moved forward until he stood between Chase and Kim. "I'm going to let memories go and invite you both inside. Separate chairs on opposite ends of the desk. We have a business meeting to conduct."

Kim scooted by Slade, hesitating as she reached the front door. Glancing over her shoulder, she hoped the warmth threatening to swarm her halted before it got within her flimsy shielding attempt. Heat of volcanic temperatures sizzled and oozed off Chase and Slade in ways that caused her body to react. Hiding taut nipples wasn't worth plucking at her top. Her mons' wetness was hidden. Well hidden under her jeans and bikini panties. How long that would stay stashed, she wasn't taking bets on that?

Kim entered the farmhouse, not checking if Slade and Chase were following her.

Slade closed the space between him and Chase. "Sorry to burst your challenge bubble."

Chase grinned. "Nothing burst. Leopards hunt by smell and sight. My eyes detected Kim's reaction. Memories don't listen well. My cock rose to the occasion. I tried thinking about last winter's snow drift I ended up in leading the sled rides down the old barn's hay chute."

Slade chuckled. "Yeah, visualizations didn't work for me either. I won't say what did come to mind. Business before pleasure or is that leisure?"

Chase patted Slade's arm as he moved forward. "I don't think leisure is on the agenda, spoken or unspoken. The over-the-shoulder glare we got said don't try it."

"I don't think our mild, meek lady is present. Certainly a more determined perhaps dominant mode instead. We'll see what comes out of our meeting," Slade offered, following Chase into the farmhouse.

Kim dropped into the chair behind the desk. She laid her courier bag on the desk and began taking out her portfolio. She glanced up as Slade and Chase entered. Kim pointed to the two chairs on opposite sides of the desk.

"Your seats await. Sort out what you need." Kim pushed the stack of papers and items toward the front of the desk, rapped on the desk, and flipped her portfolio open. "Meeting is called to order."

Slade dropped into the chair closest to her. Kim flipped through her notes. She snuck a sideways glance at Chase. He picked up two of the pads and walked away from the desk. Running away? She wet her lips and glanced at Slade. He watched her. Intently watched her. Watched her with a keen hunter's assessment. That stare still reminded her of the coyote wolf dog she'd seen at the Chicago Zoo. Intelligent and sizing up those watching him at the same time.

"If you two are done," Chase began, dragging two flip chart stands across the room. "Putting things down in front of us—on paper each of us gets to keep or take pictures of—is a sure-fire way to keep things focused and on point."

Slade shoved his chair away from the desk, laughing and picking up a marker close to the edge of the desk. "Let's not revert to tic-tac-toe contest or Pictionary, okay?"

Kim coughed, snorted, and shook her head. "Okay, we've burst the balloons twice over. I'm here on business. Owens needs wines. Local wines. I bought Owens because local businesses are what keep Sylvan Valley and Cauldron Falls thriving. Sure, we get the tourists from out of the area from time to time. But we're the next generation. The next ones to leave a place where we can grow old and still thrive. Shining as we coffee klatch. Gathering in the park for corn hole tournaments and family reunions."

"True," Chase said, drawing two squares on one flip pad he placed on the stands. "As lifestyle choices change and acceptance spreads, we can't hide anymore. Zach told me that the paper's subscriptions are growing to include Nashville, Chattanooga and even Chicago."

Slade uncapped his marker. He added three triangles inside the square. "Square represents Cauldron Falls and Sylvan Valley. Each triangle is a cluster. Neighborhoods. There are more. Dealing with the largest ones would add five to six more triangles. How do we bring in outside business? More citizens who want to live and enjoy what we offer. Acceptance, tolerance and a place or places to enjoy daily life."

Chase drew another square on the second flip chart. He drew seven columns and four rows. "Sadie Hawkins events bring in business. Problem is full moon events ebb and flow like the seasons. Full moons each month. New moons, too. Is there another way we could attract people?"

Kim reached for the remaining group of markers. She drew one in particular. She walked over to Chase's drawing and drew a red circle. She wrote one word in capital letters below it and enclosed it in a rectangle. She stepped back and tossed the marker on the desk. "Eclipse."

"Eclipse?" Slade asked, sitting in the chair close to the flip charts.

"Daytime ones?" Chase pulled the other chair next to Slade and sat.

"Maybe. The one I'm focusing on is in a week. Time to advertise and draw a crowd." Kim tapped the flip chart. "Red moon eclipse. Blood red moon eclipse, aka a Hunter Moon."

"That's not happening in our area." Chase turned sideways in his chair. "Daytime event that most are going to ignore."

"Not if we broadcast the event inside. Say, Owens' dining room?" Kim pulled the desk chair over to where Chase and Slade sat. She positioned the chair in front of them. "I've got friends that can remote us in on the satellite feed happening in Europe and Asia. Time in Chicago took me away to meeting unique people. Magics, supernatural and other humans that live knowing there's more to life than just the five senses."

Chase laughed. "You mean more than mortal. Aka human five senses."

Kim pointed at him, shaking her head. "Duality gives you and Slade shared experiences with your animal and magic parts. Me—I got so many different bits and pieces. Sometimes I wonder if I'm not like a damn card deck. Fifty-two different things all vying for dominance. Learning to quell them into a cohesive group isn't easy."

Slade stood. "All right. We got an idea. How are we going to bring it off?"

Kim rapped on the arm of her chair. "Damn it, Slade. I said broadcast the eclipse. We need place to set up viewing screens, food, drink and probably accommodations for those that imbibe more than safe driving allows."

Chase scooted his chair between Slade and Kim. His turn at peacekeeper. "Hey, you two. What about this? Lunch at Owens. A shuttle bus to the winery and a post-lunch happy hour watching the eclipse and. . ." Chase stopped speaking. He wondered if Kim's aunt and her business partner would be willing to take on his next idea on short notice.

Slade turned away from Kim. Chase slowly exhaled. Five years ago, they'd been yelling at each other. Scrapping like a couple of cats fighting over a few inches of fence. And the rest of the whole damn fence was still open for pissing on and claiming.

"Okay, Chase. You got our attention. What's your idea?" Slade held out a pen. "Flip the sheet and let's outline this."

Chase stepped around Slade and picked up a different marker. "I'm choosing purple. My fave color and one that stands out from the others we've used."

Chase flipped sheets on each flip chart and faced Kim and Slade. "We set up the old bunk house into a series of compact hostel rooms. Ones that could be suites or single rooms. If folks want to have afternoon delight or even into the next few days, the bunk house is available and we price it as part of the eclipse matchmaking event."

Slade scowled at him. "You saying offer orgy rooms for a fee?'

Kim laughed. "If they want to have an orgy, none of our or your business. Cuz they're all going to be adults. Remember—no forget that part of things."

"Can't stop the memories igniting, darlin. We had our times with those desires, too. Had some damn fine personal orgies." Slade grinned, rubbing his hands together. "We could try out the bunk house accommodations and see how they work out."

Chase tapped on the flip chart closest to him. "Business first. Then maybe pleasure."

Kim and Slade flipped their middle fingers at him. Both hands worth. Chase turned, pressing his lips together. Mirth threatened to erupt. Goddess above, they were dancing around the attraction heat dancing through and around them. He'd melted the snow drift in his mind four times over. Could admitting their attraction clear the air? Not likely, but it might cool the pheromones and hormones trying to drag the meeting in their direction.

"There's too many things dancing around in here. I'm going to clear part of it away." Chase faced Kim and Slade. "We've had some glorious threesomes in the past. I've got memories percolating being here together. I'm not sure we're ready to have one again. I'm focusing on business."

Kim tossed her portfolio on the desk. She stood, walked over to Slade, and leaned down until her forehead rested close to his. "Slade Stoneworth, stop stirring up my, your and Chase's gonads. You got your blow job last time we were together. Chase got his, too. We didn't fuck cuz it was my time of month. We ran out of condoms."

Kim straightened, paced toward Chase until they were toe-to-toe. "You Chase Blackstone are oozing and tomcatting like you're claiming some feline in heat. I'm not in heat. I appreciate your frankness. Think about sitting on a cake of ice for the rest of this meeting, okay?"

Kim dropped back into the office chair. She cleared her throat, ready to comment on Chase's earlier suggestion.

"Alert! Alert! Alert!" blasted out of each of the three cell phones laying on the desk. Three buzzes blared. More buzzes sounded. Each growing in volume.

Kim rushed to the desk, grabbed her cell phone, and entered her code to unlock it. Chase next to her, looking at his. Slade entering info on his as well. Three more buzzes and alerts sounded. She looked down.

Lightning flashed. Thunder boomed. Lights blinked.

"What the hell?" Kim blinked. Pitch black darkness. Only the glow of three blinking and buzzing cell phones illuminated her, Chase, and Slade's faces.

"Atmospheric incident." Chase leaned toward her, showing the message on his phone screen. "Wind sheers and moisture mixing. Hail, thunderstorms, and strong winds for the next six to eight hours. Tornado watch in effect."

"I guess this meeting is called due to weather." Kim stuffed her portfolio in her courier bag. "I gotta get going. Make it back to Owens."

"Rain is coming down hard. Police and weather officials are saying shelter in place until the storm passes. You are here for the duration. You got a survival bag in your car?" Slade turned the flashlight on his phone on.

"Yeah. Why you asking?" Kim leaned against the desk, waiting for her night vision to kick in.

"Tornado watch means seek shelter in protected area. Basement of the bunk house is best option. Chase, grab your and my survival backpacks from the front closet. Michael left the food cart with our lunch near the back door. We can stuff one of the large canvas totes with it."

"On it Slade." Chase started toward the dimly illuminated open doorway. "You take Kim to get her bag out of her car and anything else we can use. Toss it in my van. We'll drive it to the bunk house."

Kim blinked as the lights flickered on and then off again. Lightning flashed outside. Pitch black darkness surrounded her except for the small area her cell phone flashlight illuminated. She had two chargers in her car. An emergency hand crank radio. Following Slade was her best option. Getting all the gear any of them had ready necessitated a group effort. Working together instead of individually. "Slade, stay where you are until I locate you. We'll make a dash for my car. Do we need to grab stuff from your car?"

"My car is in the garage at the bunkhouse. We'll pull your car into the garage next to the office. Chase's van is right outside the garage." Slade held out his hand as she got closer. "Grab my hand. We'll deal with hormones later. I've got a flashlight next to the front door. We need to go now before the wind picks up again."

"Grab the two rain ponchos near the door," Chase called out. "I'm making a dash for the back door with our backpacks and the food."

Slade gripped her hand. Heat shot across her palm digging its way into her wrist and inching up her forearm. Kim tried to pull her hand away. Slade tightened his grip. "I feel it, too. Not the time to react. We need to act."

Lightning sliced through the air, striking the ground close to the front porch. Slade let go of her hand. He pulled both rain ponchos off the coat hooks near the door. "We've got about two minutes to dash to your car and move it. Got your car keys handy?"

Kim bunched up the poncho and pulled it over her head. "In my pocket. Did Chase get my tote?"

"Yes. Saw him sling it over his shoulder as the lights flashed." Slade opened the door more. Another blast of thunder rumbled as more lightning flashed. "Come on. It's now or we're stuck here."

Slade seized her hand and started out the door. Kim gritted her teeth as another blast of hormonal heat raced up and down her arm. Storms inside and out. Which one did she ignore? Could she ignore either one? Getting safely from the porch to her car and into Chase's van after they parked in the garage was going to be a minor magical feat. Were their individual deities ready to help them?

CHAPTER FOUR

Two more lightning bolts split the sky followed by loud thunder that rattled the garage's metal roof. Kim slinked further back into the garage wondering if Slade and she made the right choice driving her car to the bunkhouse. As the storm paused, she caught sight of Chase driving his van behind them. The dark bunkhouse loomed against the blackened sky with each lightning burst. Another thunderclap shook the roof as the wind whistled through the open spaces and rushed around them pushing them forward. Kim gripped the passenger side door handle. She managed to tune in a brief weather update on the car radio as they drove to the bunkhouse. A lull in the storm front was due in the next few minutes. Could they unpack and make it inside before the derecho hit them?

"Grab what you can and stash as much as you can in things," Slade called out. "There's two trash bins at the front of the garage. Toss what needs to go in. Hurry."

Kim turned as a beam from the flashlight Slade held illuminated the two bins. Flip lids might keep the contents dry if the wind didn't kick up. She dragged the bin closest to her, past the passenger rear door, and stopped. She opened the door and reached inside. Slade and the flashlight were already lighting the items. Kim tossed her survival emergency duffel in first. Next went the plastic cases holding chargers and the crank emergency radio. Two bags of clothes she'd forgotten to drop off at the local thrift store and a pair of old sneakers. Slade leaned toward her holding out the flashlight. "Hold this please, while I clear out this side and get the trunk. Anything in the front you need?"

"I'll grab the insurance papers in a moment." Kim shined the flashlight on the backseat where Slade groped for items. He chuckled as he held up two stuffed animals her niece and nephew left in the car their last visit. Slade tossed them in the bin. "Never know when these might come in handy."

"Okay seat is empty. Let me grab the registration and insurance papers." Kim closed the passenger rear door. She flipped open the glove compartment, grabbed the large envelope holding the owner's manual, registration, and insurance papers.

"Trunk's open. Lock the doors. What do we need out of the trunk?" Slade shined the light across the items.

"Grab the bag close to you. Got rubber boots, old coats, and hats. Glad I didn't get to the thrift store. We can probably use them to keep warm if the electric goes out." Kim stashed the roll of trash bags in her bin and flipped the bin's lid closed.

Slade grabbed the toolbox and slammed the trunk closed. "Tools can be used a myriad of ways. Come on, the wind is picking up."

Kim edged her way to the edge of the open garage door. Wind swept in, whistled around her, and nudged her closer to the outside. Slade tossed his flashlight in his bin, flipped the lid closed and clasped her hand. "Come on. Mad dash to the porch and door."

Thunder mixed with more lightning as rain began pelting them as they reached the bunkhouse porch steps. Slade motioned her closer. "Go on up. The door should be unlocked. Chase passed us as we pulled into the garage. He probably parked in the second garage behind the bunkhouse."

Kim turned ready to walk backwards up the steps pulling her trash bin with her. Slade grabbed the handle. His hand brushing hers. He looked down, back up at her and grinned. "Hope that heat keeps growing and glowing. Gonna need it if it gets much chillier. I've got both bins. Go on and get the door open."

The door swung open, thudding against the outside wall as she reached the top step. Chase stepped out. "Got the van unloaded. Let's get the rest inside. Power's out. We're gonna be roughing it. Hope you remember how to camp."

Kim pressed her lips firmly against each other, swallowed her retort and entered the bunkhouse. The last time they'd gone camping an unexpected threesome resulted. Were the powers-that-be playing poker with loaded dice as they bet on the next hand's outcome?

Slade pulled one of the trash bins up onto the porch. "Camp out. Lupa help us. Who's gonna chaperone this time? Your cousins aren't in the next tent waiting to catch us like our last campout."

Chase shrugged. "Who says what happened last time is going to repeat? Or even get a spark ignited?"

"Your phermones. My phermones. Kim's too. And the heat sizzling off her and me when we touched." Slade hesitated close to the open door. "You missed that when you touched her?"

"Scalded me like hot water popping out of a boiling pan. Warped its way across my palm and refused to cool down." Chase yanked the other bin up the steps. "Blatant enough for you?"

Slade shook his head. "I gave up fucking. No satisfaction beyond the temporary release. I can do that jacking off."

Chase faced Slade. "My leopard feeds off emotional energy. Mating is okay. End result involving heart and psyche is a thunderous reward and energy blast. Never could fuck. Didn't understand it in puberty and still don't."

"Let's get inside before the storm worsens. We've got a bonfire of emotions, hormones and attraction happening at a lot of levels." Slade pushed his bin into the bunkhouse, checking Chase followed him.

Kim sat on the couch middle of the expansive living room. In between lightning flashes, she could make out other pieces of furniture. A large table sat toward the back left half of the room. Possibly close to the kitchen. Wall immediately in front of the couch emitted smoky smells. A fireplace? Wet woodsy smells mixed with the smoky ones. Had Chase brought in firewood? Was there a flue that needed closing? Maybe a grate that they could use for cooking?

"Way rain's coming down and the wind blowing, we're here for a day, maybe two." Chase bumped the couch with the bin he pushed forward in the darkness.

"Good thing we restocked the can goods. Michael said the restock included canned meat and tuna." Slade's breath warmed her neck.

Kim slowly turned, wishing her night vision would clear. Neither of her night totems seemed to be paying attention. She chafed her arms. Night tremors threatened to swamp her. "Are we stuck in the basement?"

"Not unless we find a way to illuminate it." Chase clasped her hand. His tone echoed her lingering psyche shove attempting to steal her peace away. Pieces of old memories could stay where she'd stashed them. In the past, in a receptacle labeled don't give a shit. That's where she needed them to remain. Tearing anything more apart wasn't going to change what happened.

"Wind isn't as strong as first storm was. Probably need to listen to weather report and determine what we do next. The basement fireplace flue connects with the main one here. I think we will be okay as long as we're close together. This place has withstood other storms and blizzards." Slade's hand rested on her shoulder. Twin bursts of heat wandered over and across her neck and reached down toward her nipples and areola. Dang feelies could keep their business elsewhere.

"Sleeping close to each other is a priority." Chase pushed one of the bins around the couch. "Mattress from the sleeper sofa and cushions from the other couches side by side. Sleeping bags, sheets, and pillows."

"Agreed," Slade said, perching on the arm of the couch. "Where is the best place? Safest place? Allow for water, toilet, and space in case we need to hunker down."

Kim heaved a sigh. Yes, she was going to add the obvious. Someone had to. "And close the door if needed. Keep the wind and water out. Us safe, dry, and able to escape as needed."

"There's a storage room on the first level mountainside of the bunkhouse. That'll slow the winds down some. There's a sink, toilet, and makeshift shower in there." Slade clicked on his flashlight. "Best get the local weather and go from there."

"Emergency radio is in my bin." Kim clicked on her cell phone flashlight. The beam flickered. Battery level showed needed charging.

"Beams over here, please," Chase called out, flipping both bins open. Kim and Slade shined their beams toward Chase.

"Found it." Chase clicked the radio on and started cranking. "I think we need to focus on best options and get with organizing."

Crackles and voices emitted from the radio. Chase stopped cranking as the crackling stopped and the announcer was clearer.

"Good evening, Sylvan Valley and Cauldron Falls. This is emergency station WXNP out of Memphis. Derecho watch is over. The storm broke up as it reached the mountains. Thunderstorms, heavy rain, and wind gusts up to thirty-five miles an hour are expected for the rest of the night and into tomorrow. Tornado Warning is downgraded to a watch for areas north and east of the area. Local and state officials encourage everyone to stay indoors, off the roads and be ready to take shelter as needed. Next broadcast in three hours or sooner if needed. WXNP over and out."

"Okay, I think we know where we're bunking." Chase stashed the emergency radio in the bin and flipped the lid closed. "Storage room is best option. Sturdy. Space to spread out some. Stay dry and not too chilly."

"Didn't Michael say that was the old kitchen at one time?" Slade stashed three small pillows off the couch in the bin close to him. "I think he found the flue connection to the old cookstove stored in there."

"We don't have electric. We need to eat. Need to keep food chilled. And us warm. How about we get moving things and decide how many layers once we're in there?" Kim stood up. "Cranking the radio to charge cell phones is going to take time. We could tell stories. Do something taking turns."

"Taking turns doing what?" Chase asked. Slade's snort and snicker weren't helping the chills running up and down Kim's arms.

"Cranking the radio. I'm for putting layers on and getting into the sleeping bags." Kim rubbed her arms briskly. "Extra flashlight available?"

A chilled hand wrapped around her wrist, tugging her sideways, and—Kim let out a high-pitched yip and swung toward the way she was leaning.

"Hey. No roughing up the dude that's got the flashlight for you." Chase clicked the flashlight on. "Damn, you got a power punch."

Kim shook her hand a bit. She grabbed the flashlight and shook it at Chase. "Let's get something straight. None of us needs to spook or scare the shit out of each other, okay?"

Slade's muffled snickers sounded slightly behind her. "That includes you, Slade. I kick dudes in the balls. Scratch and bite. Toss in a couple head buts and punches. I don't play."

"Honey, none of us ever got that damn kinky or wild. Nips, a few swats, and clothespins on nipples and occasionally your clit." Slade coughed shutting Chase up.

"Memories, gents. Memories." Kim gave a few tsk-tsks and arced the flashlight beam over the walls as she turned around. "I'm adding that it's too damn damp and chilly to argue about fucking sex."

"Glad to know you aren't into fucking," Slade quipped, shoving a bin past Kim. "Doorway you're looking for is right behind you."

Kim spun around, shone the beam straight ahead. The partially open door came into focus. The darkness behind the open door inched toward her if she let her imagination run wild. Let her memories of a dark midnight in a tent in two double sleeping bags zipped together. Two males and her. One male on either side of her. Deity, was another night like the one beckoning them into its lurid cascade of—oh hell no, she wasn't jumping into bed with either

Chase or Slade. Or even both of them. There was attraction, horny hormones, and percolating pheromones. All of her could turn on their air conditioning. "Chase, you got one chance to smart ass comment. Better take it now."

Chase cleared his throat twice. Stepped into the flashlight beam and said, "Honey, none of us ever were fuckers. Suckers possibly. I'm leaving that be. I'll finish with if cuddling and sharing body warmth is on tonight's agenda, I'm all for it. Clothed cuddling. Too damn damp and chilly for much more!"

"Who's gonna check things out first?" Kim kept trying to shine the flashlight beyond the door into the opening leading into the room.

"Darlin'," Slade whispered, creeping closer to Kim, "you could do the honors."

Chase snickered. "Slade, stop with scare stuff. I checked out the room last week. There's room in there for all our stuff. Shelf space to put it on. The old flue is workable. Michael and I put some kindling and wood in there along with a couple bags of wood chips and pellets. The outside door to the external grill needs a locksmith to get the door open and lock fixed."

"Damn, Chase," Slade scolded. "Getting Kim to snuggle close and. . ."

"Ouch!" Slade yelped. "What did you do that for?"

Kim laughed. "Warmed your ass for you and letting you know it's paybacks now or would you prefer after we're settled in for the night? You get the sleeping bag zipper chilling against you."

"Not doing doubled up!" Slade chuckled. "Side by side, okay. May have to zip sleeping bags together to make top and bottom covers. We'll see what we got."

"Ain't any of us getting buckass naked either." Chase chafed his arms. "Chill is settling in. I turned the tap on in the kitchen. Don't expect to freeze overnight. Might frost."

Kim shone her flashlight at the open door. "Come on, let's get what we know is movable in there and check things out."

Wind buffeted the outside, whistling and rattling anything caught in its path. Rain poured against the dwindling daylight. Kim strode forward, praying her vivid imagination would stop tickling her memories and poking her psyche. She did not need daymares, erotic memories creeping up or nightmares conjuring.

She paused outside the door, standing at the entrance to the unknown and leaving her imaginary fears and qualms outside. They pooled around her knees and feet pushing, crying to go with her. They made their icy presence known, running their shiver-causing tendrils up and down her legs and feet.

One more step and across the door's threshold she'd be. Inside and the unknown became known. Kim inhaled and exhaled twice and shoved the door open. A loud thud and rattling sounded. Dust and dirt littered the air as she moved deeper into the storage room. Rattling sounded as the wind whipped around the side of the bunkhouse. She moved toward the loudest rattle. Cool air reached out to her as the small grill area came into view. The external door budged and rattled with each wind buffet.

Shining the flashlight around the grill, there were no mice or rodent droppings. A small rear door showed where the cold air and wind entered. Kim leaned forward, grasped the door's handle, and shoved the door closed. The wind pushed back against her. A tug of war in the making. Kim hoped the few magic phrases she knew calmed the air between the inner and outer door, giving her the space to latch the two together. "Calm between the doors happen now. Stillness I call forth. Be mine in the next few moments."

Quiet, followed by silence, eeked its way into the space between the doors. Pressure pummelled the outside door causing creaks and groans as the wood held firm and the spell energy didn't grow or move. Kim hastily shoved the interior door closed, pressing her palm against the door and envisioning it solidly latching in place. A small click sounded and both doors rattled as the wind pushed against the outside.

She stepped back, catching her bottom lip between her teeth as angst and suspicion rolled off her. The wind died down as more rain pounded against the outside walls. A high-pitched ringing began in one ear as one thought flashed through her mind. *You're safe. Be at peace. Bask in the now.* What was the now? She wasn't sure. Experiencing it would reveal what the now was. She hoped her do, grow and learn part of it made sense.

CHAPTER FIVE

"I don't know what happened in here," Chase spoke from behind Kim. "I'm not sure I want to know."

Kim faced Chase. "One of those tutorial things I learned in Chicago. A bit of witchery. A tad of magic and a whole lot of hoping and praying."

"Mixture worked well. Thanks for doing that." Slade wheeled one of the bins into the room. "Let's get a couple lanterns lit. I think we can get the cushions and mattress in here with room to spare."

Chase located one of the lanterns. The click of a switch sounded. The lantern's soft light filled parts of the room. Items lining shelves took on ghostly appearances as their shadows painted their existence across the floor and close by walls. "Slade, the other lantern is on the first shelf behind you."

Slade pushed the bin to the center of the room. He clicked the second lantern's switch. Light reached up to the ceiling and illuminated more of the walls and floor. "Are there more batteries?"

"Kim, shine your cell phone over here, please." Chase moved back.

Kim pointed her phone toward the shelves and lantern. She could make out boxes, cans, pots, and pans. Name and items came into view the closer she got. "Looks like we got dried goods. Canned items and pots. Great. We need a can opener and utensils."

"Let's get the things in here. We can explore afterward." Slade started back toward the door holding the lantern he lit.

"Easier said than done," Chase called out. "Kim needs to shut her cell phone off. Where did you put your flashlight?"

"In the bin," Slade called back. "Should be on top."

"Still the same old Slade. Give orders and walk off to do what he thinks is best," Kim muttered.

"Them alpha genes. No denying them. He's right though we do need to get settled before it gets too dark." Chase opened the bin, held the lantern aloft and peered inside the bin. "Kim, flashlight's right on top. Can you grab it, please?"

Kim shuddered. The last time she'd reached into something barely illuminated, she'd damn near grabbed a fucking rubber snake. Her stupid cousins didn't check to see if a real snake had coiled up next to the fake jobber.

She wasn't taking a chance on getting bit. "Only if you hold the lantern so I can easily see the flashlight and the area around it. I don't need any more surprises."

"None of us do." Chase held the lantern closer to the bin. "Best I can do."

Kim flexed her hand, inhaled and—Cold metal met her palm. She kept her eye on the cylinder she wrapped her fingers around while noting where Chase stood. Getting burned from the lantern wasn't on her agenda in this lifetime or any other. "Got it. Slowly move back as I get it out, please."

Chase shuffled close to her. The edge of the lantern's circle of light shifted from the bin's interior to the edge of it. Kim drew her hand up and out of the bin rapidly. She shook and spun around. "Okay, turning it on."

Chase nodded as the flashlight beam outlined him. He set the lantern on the floor. "Great job. And I shuddered too. Nothing like being scared of the bloody dark. My leopard vision is good to a point. Not the best when the damn darkness is tossing illusions and apparitions at me mentally."

"Yeah, your inner kid reaches out and gooses you," Slade whispered right behind them.

Screams and yelps echoed off the walls and ceiling.

"Damn it Slade! No fair!" Kim and Chase yelled almost simultaneously.

Slade jumped back, just missing Kim's punch and Chase's kick. "I fouled! No more kicking and punching, please."

"How about we agree to stop aiding our imaginations? Work together to get settled for the night?" Chase picked up the lantern and set it on the counter close to him.

"Agreed," Slade said, setting his lantern next to Chase's. "I found utensils, potholders, a can opener, and a few towels in the kitchen. They're on the shelf next to the pans."

"Let's get the rest in here. That last thunderclap didn't sound too far off." Chase started toward the door holding his lantern.

Kim followed Chase. "Slade, you can stand here in the semi dark letting your kid minions tickle your repressed memories or you can haul your ass along with us to help out."

Four more trips back and forth from the living room to the storage room brought the bulk of the items inside. Kim rubbed her hands together. Chilly air reached out into the room more as darkness fell outside. Thunder and lightning bursts crackled and boomed, echoing off the nearby mountains and buildings.

How much more she could withstand before hangry and cold took over, she wasn't sure.

"I checked out the makeshift bathroom. Water is cold. Toilet is flushable. Suggest heat water for washup after we get some food and hot drinks consumed." Slade knocked on the metal pipe he found examining the bathroom. "Might be woodstove."

Chase clicked on the extra flashlight they found going through the kitchen drawers on their last foraging trip. He moved the beam up and down the wall. A large dark item came into view. "Does look like a stove. Makes better use than trying to use the grates we found connecting with the outside grill."

Slade banged on the metal his hand slid over. Echoes sounded and faded. "Let's see if we can get the door open and a fire going. We got plenty of wood."

"Don't we need to open the flue? Don't need to smoke ourselves." Kim rummaged in one of the donation bags. She held up three sweatshirts. "I call first dibs."

Chase grabbed one, pulled it on and glanced at the saying. "Women roar the best. Yup, they sure do. Depends on what you got them roaring about."

Kim shook her head and tossed a sweatshirt at Slade. "You can turn it inside out if feminine power disturbs your male qi energy."

"Hey, we're all halves of each sex. Took a female and a male to make us." Slade slipped the sweatshirt on. "I'm taking warm over cold. Thank you for getting these out."

Kim hastily pulled hers on. She rubbed her arms twice and stomped her feet. "All right, let's see what's with this stove. I'm hungry and ready to gnaw on something. It ain't gonna be either of you. So behave!"

More knocks and pings sounded as each of them tapped and rapped on the stove. Kim slid her hand down the area she stood close to. A cold, coiled metal item caressed her palm. She gripped the coil and tugged as she moved shining the flashlight downward. Bits of dust and dirt filled the air and vanished. Blasts of chilled air rushed out, billowing their way up and down her face and chest. "I found the door."

"Awesome." Chase set his lantern on top of the stove. "Air coming out indicates the flue is open. I think I found the flue pipe shutter crank." Chase turned the crank toward the wall. "Did the air flow stop?"

Kim waved her hand up and down. The air chill lessened some. "Still some. Turn the crank opposite direction."

Chase turned the crank back toward him. "What about now?"

"Damn, that's cold." Kim moved away from the open door. "Okay, we know how that works. Is there enough wood to get a cooking fire going?"

"Enough to get us through a couple of days." Slade brushed past her carrying two large wood chunks, some kindling, and a scoop.

"We got the lunch Michael brought over. We need to eat that and get ready to sleep. I saw a coffee pot. I can rinse it out and put the tea to warm in it." Chase set his lantern on the counter next to the sink. He turned the faucet on. The pipes groaned and spat out a trickle of water. Chase stuck his fingers in the flow and held them up to the light. "Gonna have to run a bit before the tap is clear to use."

"What about the jugs we saw in the kitchen? We can fill those and get them in here while the tap runs." Slade looked up as another clap of thunder rattled the roof. "It's gonna be a quick trip for sure. Needs all of us carrying two jugs each."

"Each carries a couple jugs and push them on the cart for extras. I say we go now." Kim was out the door pushing the cart.

Chase looked at Slade. Slade shrugged and started toward the door. "Gotta admire her grit. I ain't gonna let her give me, I told you. I'm going with her."

Chase grabbed the coffee pot and bolted out the storeroom door following Slade and Kim.

Kim laid her flashlight on the cart and quickly maneuvered around the couch and chairs. Two lightning bolts and a clap of thunder reverberated off the kitchen walls as she entered. Water attracted electricity and that lightning was bright. It could damn well stay outside and away from the bunkhouse. She saw the jugs on the counter close to the sink. She grabbed two, took the lids off, turned on the water, and rinsed both jugs out.

"Keep rinsing. I'll put the caps or lids on the cart so we can close them once they're full." Slade set two more jugs on the counter.

Kim rinsed and filled all four. Slade set them on the cart. A rumble of thunder sounded close by. "Shit, we gotta hurry. Don't need lightning zapping us or the bunkhouse."

Chase entered the kitchen as Slade capped the last of the four jugs. "Fill three more. I'm rinsing out the coffee pot in the prep sink."

Kim rinsed, filled, and set each of the three remaining jugs on the cart. Slade quickly capped them. More thunder sounded closer like it was practically over the bunk house. "Chase, hurry we gotta turn the water off.'

"Done. I turned the tap off in the storeroom. We've got enough water to keep us for the night and tomorrow. Let's go." Chase grabbed the coffee pot, turned off the faucet, and trotted past Kim and Slade.

Slade followed Chase pushing the cart. Kim didn't hesitate. She ran out of the kitchen. She passed Chase and Slade. "Come on. I hope we're safe in there."

Chase held up the book he'd swept off the corner table as he entered the storeroom. "Picture and written history of the bunk house. I think there's lightning rods on the roof. We'll find out once we get settled."

Kim unloaded the cart while Chase and Slade dragged cushions and sofa sleeper mattress into the room. Chase dropped down on one set of cushions and cranked the emergency radio. He turned up the volume and continued cranking.

"Happy evening folks. This is WXNP. The eye of the storm is north of Cauldron Falls and Sylvan Valley. Local authorities and state officials are asking everyone to shelter in place. The next twelve hours are going to be time to rest, eat and grab some sleep. Winds are dying down. Local flooding is happening. Be safe. Stay put until daylight. Next broadcast is in three hours. This is WXNP Memphis over and out."

Chase set the radio on the floor beside him. "Sounds like we've gotten through the worst. Cooped up together for the next couple of days isn't going to be bad."

Slade chuckled. "Depends on how you define bad."

Kim clapped. "Now, we're all focused again. Let's stop with the woes and figure out the blessings. We're safe. We worked things out to keep food going, water available, and even wash up. I'd say basic necessities beyond the toilet."

Chase groaned. "Seems we always come back to the group naked things again."

"*Naked what?*" Kim spat out. "Nowhere was that word bantered about!"

"I think," Slade began between laughs. "Chase bantered it this time."

Chase stood. "Naked, three of us and doing stuff is the elephant in the damn room. There's not enough room for the blasted pachyderm in here with us!"

Kim inhaled, held her breath, and blew air out through her open mouth. Things had come full circle. Storm forced them together. Business brought them together. Surviving turned on their cooperation and now . . .Craptastic was lighting off fireworks.

"All right. We're here. The damn issue acknowledged. Before hangry and cold dominate us. Let's get a fire going. Tea heating, food warming if needed, and situate the sleeping area." Kim walked toward the makeshift bathroom. "I'm making room for tea and food. You can turn your head or ignore the door doesn't appear to fully close."

Chase picked up the lantern close to him. "Slade, let's get the sleeping area laid out."

Slade glanced toward the darken area Kim had walked into. He shook his head and faced Chase. "Challenge issued. We expect the same in return. Let's get our part done."

Kim finished emptying her bladder. The roll of dry old toilet paper crumpled in her hand. She used more, hoping there was something else they could use. She dried and tossed the damp wad in the trash can she kicked as she sat down. Time to fuss and ignore the pheromones and hormones flying by slapping them, tantalizing them, and signaling their nethers that doing it wasn't going to be ignored. Washing up would take some of the water. Letting the tap run would provide water to wash up with. Keeping warm was going to be a three-body night. Could they put on enough clothes to stave off chills and convince their gonads that shucking clothes and going for it had to wait? She wasn't crossing her fingers and toes on that one. She wasn't betting on those odds either.

"When you're done, I'm next," Chase said. "Tea is warming. Sandwiches are warming."

"I'm done." Kim stepped into the circle of light the two lanterns cast side by side, close to the center of the room. "Need to wash my hands. In my survival bag is liquid hand soap."

"I'll get it." Slade shone his flashlight into the bin closest to him. "The fire is small for now. Any thermal underwear or sweatpants in those donation bags?"

Kim reached for the flashlight Slade held. Her hand grazed his. Sparks jumped from her hand to his and his to hers. She worried her bottom lip and gripped the flashlight tighter. "Might be. Know there are jeggings and leggings in there. Those don't have flies."

Slade held the bottle of liquid hand soap up. "Lupa and Deity! Thrown together and gotta wear damn chastity belts to sleep in. The stories we'll have to tell when this is over."

"No telling happening." Kim tossed three items on the mattress. "Last time our story got out, the fill-ins and gossip add-ons had more bullshit happening than a pasture full of cattle produce."

Slade snickered. "True. What you throw on the mattress?"

Chase grabbed an item and held it up. "Sweatpants! I call dibs!"

Slade reached for one of the remaining items. "Hoping for more sweatpants. Don't care if they're frilly girly colors either!"

Kim pulled the two items out of Slade's reach. "Both are sweatpants. I think they're hot pink."

Slade glanced at Chase. "You gonna tell me what color you got?"

"Nope, cuz it's too damn cold to worry about color. Ain't nobody gonna see or know except us." Chase slipped past Slade. "My turn to empty my bladder. I say warming up some wash-up water is our next chore after we eat."

Slade tossed the sweatpants Kim handed him on the counter behind him. "Sleep arrangements are three people huddling together. Sleeping bags and small throw pillows. Finest accommodations we have to offer, ma'am."

Kim sighed. "And each of us wearing two to three layers. Gonna make shucking clothes for much of anything pretty impossible."

"Sighing because you hoping for more?" Slade moved closer to Kim.

Kim burst out laughing. "More? More's not going to happen until it's a hell of a lot warmer and a lot of talking been done."

"I think we got most of the talking part handled." Chase's laughter reached them. "Yeah, eavesdropping while piddling."

Slade and Kim's laughter joined Chase's.

Slade used the toilet next. Kim sniffed the air. "Damn you are aromatic."

"Never said I didn't stink at times." The low flush of the toilet sounded. "I'll add water in a moment to it."

"Good thing you checked before you did that." Chase bumped Slade with a pan filled with water. "Here you go."

More laughter followed. Kim wiped her eyes. "We know each other's funny bones for sure."

"Good thing. Helps clear out the silence ice we don't need and the nattering anger energy hiding our fears and uneasiness." Chase put three mugs on the counter next to the stove. "Tea and sandwiches are ready."

Slade filled the pan he used with water. "Soap is next to the sink. Water to wet hands. Tap on to rinse and towel to dry."

Kim tossed the towel Slade handed her over her shoulder. She quickly washed and dried her hands. Chase went next. Slade last.

Fifteen minutes later, they sat cross-legged on the cushions, balancing plates holding sandwiches, some sort of chips and a couple of cookies each. Mugs of tea were on the floor close to each of them. Hunger and close-by body warmth kept their banter to a minimum as they ate. They'd all pitch in on clean up. Unasked question was who was sleeping in the middle of the sleeping bag pile? Kim wasn't sure she wanted to know. Her mind could stop tossing reminders of what happened last time she was in the middle between Chase and Slade in a prone sleeping position.

CHAPTER SIX

Kim dried the last mug and set it next to the other two. Chase was in the makeshift shower washing up. His cuss word choices were ones that she couldn't translate. Probably muffled by wind bursts buffeting the roof. Slade stood at the counter across from her, leafing through the book Chase had snatched on one of their earlier foraging raids.

"This is interesting. The remodel took place over five years. Prior owners wanted a bed and breakfast plus the vineyard. Work hands bunked here for a couple of years." Slade flipped the book over.

"Does it say what they did with the bunkbeds?" Chase asked, pulling his sweatshirt back on. "I think you know how cold it is in there."

"Cold in the bunkbeds? Or the icy chill cooling your naughty thoughts?" Slade lifted the pan holding his warmed wash water. "Hope you left some towels and soap. Hate to step on a wet, cold floor and slip."

"Floor is fine. My cold, damp towel is ready to massage the soles of your feet. Can hang towels up to dry when we're all done. That includes you, Kim." Chase dropped onto one of the cushions and pulled on socks.

"Yeah, I know. Cleaning up before bed is the best thing. Brush your teeth now or wait until we're all back in here?" Kim laid the damp dish towel out on the counter. It might be dry by morning.

"You go first." Chase laid a tube of toothpaste on the counter. "I'm checking what else is in here."

Kim finished brushing her teeth as Slade exited the bathroom. "Sorry my yelping carried out here."

Kim clapped her hand over her mouth, not wanting to spit water all over the counter. She leaned over the sink and lowered her hand. She rinsed her mouth and hands. "Slade, you still can't howl and sing on key. At least this time Chase didn't try to yowl in counter melody."

"No need to sound like we're in here dying and ill." Chase tossed the items he held on the mattress and cushions. "Scrounging around pays off. Found sheets and a couple of blankets. More warmth."

Kim picked up the lantern next to her. "All right. Here's what's happening. I'm not going in that cold, wet area. I'm washing up out here next to the stove. Some warmth. You two can make up the sleeping area."

Chase and Slade glanced at each other, grinned and shrugged. "Can't say we won't peek given an opportunity." Chase unfolded one of the sheets.

"Won't even accuse you of trying to turn us on or subtle hint you want us to notice." Slade grabbed the end of the sheet Chase fluffed in the air.

Kim dipped part of the towel she held in the water. Slade had brought out the soap after he'd hung up the towels. She quickly washed her face and neck. She checked if Slade and Chase were watching her. No. Not even covertly at the moment. She got her bra off, laid it on the counter, washed under her arms, and lowered her sweatpants enough to wash between her legs.

Goddess, she hadn't had a sink bath since she'd gotten her own place. Washing up before bed was a must growing up. Sharing a double bed with her younger sister hadn't been easy. Emily tossed and turned often ending up sprawled in the middle of the bed. Sleeping on the foot of the bed had its pluses. Like being able to scoot to the bathroom without the bed cooling down too much. Often got her first dibs on the morning bath with warm water.

"Still got a nice ass," Slade commented.

Kim pulled up her sweatpants and wrung out the towel. "Thanks. Now that bedding your two been messing with, best be ready to inspect as to who is sleeping where."

"Gonna need to zip sleeping bags together. Put 'em under us or over us. Shared body warmth helps keep heat going." Slade tucked the corners of the king-size flat sheet under the edge of the mattress and cushions. "Two on the mattress and one on the cushions."

"There might be a couple more sheets. I grabbed what I could carry." Chase held up one of the blankets. "Person in middle is going to get half of each to cover them. I think maybe we put them on top of the sheet. Another sheet over them and then sleeping bags over us."

Kim pressed her lips together, wishing her psyche would shut up. Images from her past pushed to the surface from their buried spot. They could go back there, too. She changed. From what she learned so far, Slade and Chase had changed as well. Maybe that was why they were here getting along decently.

Differently and—She wet her lips and asked the question nagging her psyche and her dang memories. "Who do you think is going to be in the middle?"

Chase dropped the sheet, laid his hand on Kim's arm, and leaned closer to her. "Slade and I are buddies. Business partners. We don't turn each other on. Middle person is you. Like before."

Slade stood. "Women turn me on. Chase is my best pal. A good business partner. Only way I mix business and pleasure is sharing a woman. Not doing Chase. Men don't light my sexual desire."

Kim swallowed twice. This wasn't a repeat of the night in the tent. Three of them crowded together, trying to have a quiet threesome. Two of their damn cousins had to walk by and kick the tent, asking in loud voices why they were so quiet in there. For the love of Lupa, it was after one a.m. that time.

"All right," Kim began, facing Slade and Chase. "I get the middle. I'm calling shots on several items then."

"We're listening." Chase unzipped two of the sleeping bags.

"Yeah, say your desires. We'll see if we can fulfill them." Slade chuckled and unzipped the third sleeping bag.

"Neither of you is capable of fulfilling the first desire." Kim grinned and reached for the sheet lying on the counter.

"Oh?" Chase quipped, working two of the zippers together.

"She's going to say she don't want the middle. No problem, she can deal with the cold zipper this time." Slade tossed his unzipped sleeping bag on the mattress.

"Nope that's not it." Kim shook the sheet out. "No protection. No sex happening. That is the first and top priority."

"Then what's the box of condoms in your survival bag for?" Slade asked, zipping his sleeping bag together with the other two.

"I don't have to answer that." Kim started to smooth the sheet on top of the blankets Chase had laid out. "Didn't know you'd taken up snooping, Slade. Or you either, Chase."

"Darlin', you think rummaging in the bins and moving them around, dumping them out and stuffing things back in isn't going to make things burst open? Push zippers past their tolerance. Like the one on these damn sleeping bags!" Chase tossed the sleeping bags on the mattress and cushions.

"What he said, and so what if you do have condoms with you. Being prepared is important. Self-care is priority. Kudos to you for doing that. Next question is are they expired." Slade picked up his lantern. "Chase and I are checking for more bedding. You coming with us?"

Kim chafed her arms twice. More covers were a plus. Putting the condoms where anyone could see them made sense. She'd have to check the date. Sex might happen come daylight. For tonight, she wasn't sure where her mind, heart and gut were. "Yes, I'm coming too. Helping out is part of TLCing each of us. Lead the way, Chase."

"Back through the pantry door and on the left side is where I found the bedding." Chase pushed the storage room door almost closed. He held up his lantern. An open door came into view. "In here."

Chase entered the small pantry. "Not much room in here."

"Good thing we got the lanterns." Slade let out a low whistle as he turned around. "Lots of stuff. Gotta get Michael out here after the storm and take inventory. See what's usable."

"I found more sheets and another blanket." Kim tapped Chase's arm. "Shine your lantern over here, please."

Two shelves held miscellaneous bedding, towels and what looked like pillows. Kim filled her arms with sheets and blankets. "Slade, can you grab the pillows?"

Slade clutched one. "Not sure how dusty they are. Maybe better to go with what we got."

"I agree." Chase lowered his lantern. "Battery is running low. We need to conserve."

"Wait a moment." Slade held his lantern close to several rounded cans. "These might be batteries we can use with the lanterns."

"Hey, there's another lantern next to them." Chase pulled the lantern to him. "Let's take it and a couple batteries. We'll see what we can do tomorrow."

Kim exited the pantry first. She inhaled and exhaled as her eyes adjusted to the semi-darkness of the storage room. Moonlight poured in through the window close to the front of the room. How could they have missed that? "Moonlight. Firelight and cozy sleeping arrangements. Guess we're destined to recreate our campout."

"Except this time I agree with you. We need to talk before any intimacy happens." Slade put the batteries on the counter away from the stove. "Let's get under the covers and crank the radio to charge cell phones. I'm not ready for sleep quite yet."

"How did we miss that window?" Kim tossed the pillows on the makeshift bed. "With the lightning, we should have seen it."

"Remember Mr. Granger, our philosophy teacher?" Chase asked, smoothing the extra blankets on top of the sleeping bags.

"Yes." Kim handed Slade a pair of fuzzy socks. "Warm feet prevent someone from getting iced as they sleep."

Slade snorted. "You got two pairs on?"

"Could you two not be so damn obvious?" Chase wet his toothbrush and put toothpaste on it. "Mr. Granger's fave phase was shoulds lead to shits. I don't mean the fertilizer type. I'm brushing my teeth. Please refrain from making me swallow toothpaste."

Kim glanced at Slade. Slade shrugged and sat on the makeshift bed. He pulled on the socks she handed him as he spoke.

"Chase, I suggest you be quick on that brushing. I'm next and don't want to swallow that stuff either." Slade grinned and winked at Kim. She shook her head.

"Thanks for reminding me about shoulds, Chase." Kim sat on the edge of the makeshift bed, pulling on her extra socks. "Mr. Granger's other fave philosophy was plans are never straight and narrow. Paths are crooked. Get used to it."

"Followed up by change is constant and juggling is a valuable trait." Slade flipped his covers back. He moved his pillow several times. "Guess I'll figure that out when we all get in."

Thunder and a wind burst sounded as Chase gargled and spit in the sink. "Guess powers that be are fussing for us to settle down."

Kim chortled. "Wish they could understand that this is not an exact replication repeat."

"My brush, gargle and spit turn." Slade chuckled as he moved past Chase. "Keep going with our topic, please."

Chase dropped down by Kim. "Thanks for turning my covers back. Hope the makeshift bed is warm and comfortable."

Kim patted her section. A good portion of the mattress. "No lumps or bumps so far. It's making sure you and Slade got enough room."

"Twin-sized for him and me. A bit of room on the mattress so we're not sleeping on the edge of the edge like that air mattress your cousins stuck us with." Chase flipped the covers over his double socked feet. "I'll get the radio in a moment and crank while we charge each of our phones."

Slade's gargle and spit sounded, followed by an off-key three-line song. "I'm not naked. Nor am I gonna be. It's too damn cold to consider it."

"Now that you announced to anyone within hearing," Chase tried to get out the rest in between snickers and snorts. "Y-you can get in bed and warm up on your own."

"I'll bring the radio." Slade shone the lantern around the floor. "Kim, where's your charger and phone?"

"On the stool, we brought in. Close to Chase's side." Kim tried to stand up. She sat back down. "I think my body is telling me stay put."

"I got it." Chase put Kim's phone in her hand. "Let's get to cranking and reminiscing or whatever it is until the phone says decently charged."

Chase connected the charger cable to the USB port. "Let me know when the phone is connected."

"All set." Kim laid the phone in her lap. "I'll take a turn cranking and tell a story or two while I do."

"I'll do the same." Slade got up. He dimmed the other lantern, set it on the counter, and turned it until it illuminated the bathroom door. "I'll crank first. Chase, you last so you can put the radio under the stool and phone on it."

Slade started cranking. "I'm going to ask a question. Why did we split up? I remember three people who were close. Good friends. Possibly even best friends. Did we cross a line that none of us acknowledged?"

"I'll," Kim began.

"I can stop cranking or keep on and finish my turn." Slade stopped speaking, kept turning and waited.

"Go ahead. I interrupted." Kim held the phone up. It glowed showing battery charging.

"Thank you." Slade kept cranking. "I didn't find out you and Chase weren't an item until you supposed eloped to Terence Spencer."

"Give your arm a rest and let me crank." Chase leaned across Kim's lap, reaching for the radio.

"Sure," Slade handed Chase the radio. "Kim, when Chase is done, it's your turn. Chase's phone is next."

Kim nodded, not caring if Chase or Slade could see her nodding. "Understood. Chase, where is your phone?"

"My phone is in one of the bins. Don't worry about charging it." Chase cranked the radio twice, flicked the on switch and cranked more. Static and quiet. Nothing more. No broadcast updates. He turned the radio off and cranked a few more times. "Q and A continue. I got back from my family reunion and cousin's wedding to find you gone, Kim. Slade wasn't speaking to me. And several of my friends were tiptoeing around me. Granted it all got better, but people acted like we were an item. Something special."

Kim held up the phone. "Almost midway. Want me to crank?"

"Not yet." Chase cranked faster. "We all got questions and unknowns. We aren't going to get it all out tonight or even tomorrow. It's going to take time."

"I'm interrupting." Kim leaned forward, stretching her back. As she leaned back, she spoke. "I didn't want to choose. I didn't know that. I thought I had to. None of our friends or close family members were in a three-way relationship. I thought what I felt was wrong. I didn't want to come between either of you. Ruin your friendship. Terrence needed a reason to get out of town. His family tried to arrange a marriage for him. Some kind of pack hierarchy set up."

"Guess the rumors about his royal blood lineage were true." Chase stopped cranking. "Kim, probably good idea to crank a bit more."

"I'll do it." Kim took the radio from Chase and began cranking. "Terrence hid something else. Before I say more, Slade, are we charging your phone?"

"No need to play hide and seek trying to find my phone." Slade laid down, adjusted his covers, and placed his pillow under his head. "I think I know what Terrence was hiding."

"I'm probably thinking the same thing." Chase pulled his covers up.

"Before either of you go off on a twenty questions chase, I'm sharing. It's known." Kim stopped cranking. She disconnected the charger from the radio and phone. She handed Chase the radio and charger. "Terrence married his college sweetheart, Zander Simons. They're happy and living in Atlanta."

Slade yawned. “Glad they’re happy. Glad we’ve talked some. I’m going to sleep. Tomorrow we’ll talk more and decide what comes next. Sound good?”

“Sleep is claiming me, too.” Kim yawned and settled under the covers. “Chase, here’s my phone.”

“Thanks Kim. Thanks Slade.” Chase put the radio under the stool and the phone on top of it. “Now we’ve gotten deeper. Tomorrow is new territory. By the way, I put the condom box under the stool in case we might need it. Good night.”

Chase dimmed the lantern. He settled under the covers. Kim turned on her back next to him. She cleared her throat. “Just cuz you put the box there don’t mean any of us agreed to something happening.”

“Ssh,” Slade said, turning on his back. “It’s mutual agreement if the box and contents are needed. Right now we sleep. That part of the campout ain’t being missed. Good night.”

CHAPTER SEVEN

Kim rolled over, squinted and shielded her eyes. Daylight poured in through the window they'd found behind the stack of linens shelf. She blinked twice and slowly lowered her hand. Sunbeams danced across the floor and partway up the wall. Bird chirps could be heard. The storm had passed?

"Good morning." Slade's voice warmed her neck and partially exposed shoulder. "Birds should learn a song that they could sing together."

"They're better than your off-key howls and yips," Chase quipped. "How did we miss that window?"

"Hidden." Kim rolled onto her back. Chase and Slade cuddled closer. "Just like us staying away from each other. Ignoring what we needed to talk about."

Chase yawned and stretched. "We stepped into the outer edge of the internal ring of what happened. Admitted some knowns. There's still more we can uncover or back away from."

"What he said." Slade sat up, stretched and yawned. "One yawns the rest do. That's contagious."

"Must be my turn." Kim covered her mouth as she yawned.

"I'm emptying my bladder. We can check the radio when I'm back." Slade tossed off his covers, stood and quickly entered the bathroom.

Chase whispered as Slade pushed the bathroom door partly closed. "Don't tell him he's wearing mismatched socks, purple sweatpants and—"

"Thank Lupa, no one else can see me. Purple sweatpants, socks that don't match and a sweatshirt that says ask me, I'm game." Slade's chuckles increase. "Never said doubt what opportunity provides. It's warm. I slept comfortably, snuggled under the covers."

Kim winked at Chase. "You know you can keep your makeshift pjs. I'm sure the thrift store donation bin won't miss them."

"I'll get back to you on that." Slade flushed the toilet. "Who's next?"

"My turn." Chase rose. "Leopard gonna disown me! Hot pink sweats with tiger paw prints on them? A sweatshirt that says ocelots do it better? My animal half is going to be giving me the stink eye."

Kim clapped her hand over her mouth. Laughter escaped. Chase's chuckles joined hers and Slade's. "Can't say we weren't warned. I don't regret being warm and cozy all night. Will take more of that for a while longer."

"Me too," Chase called out, trotting into the bathroom.

"When Chase gets back, you gotta reveal your sweats outfit and socks. I hope he doesn't look too close at his socks. He despises snakes." Slade kissed Kim's cheek.

"I heard that. These are lizards. Not snakes." The toilet rattled. "Oh, shit!"

"We don't need to know what you are doing. Your aroma will catch up to us." Slade slipped his arm around Kim's waist, hugging her to him.

"Behave. We are minus a chaperone." Kim rolled away from Slade. "Chase, whatever is on the socks don't matter. You survived. You can toss 'em back in the donation bag after you hand-wash them."

"Gee, thanks. Guess I gotta get used to handling distorted snaky lizards!" Chase closed the toilet lid with a thud. The flush sounded. Pipes creaked and groaned as water trickled into the tank. "Now I got tank fill duty."

"Look at it this way. Now you know what remodeling and plumbing needs done to turn this into an Airbnb." Slade buried his face in his pillow, laughter shaking his shoulders.

"How long do I need to hold my breath while I take my turn in there?" Kim asked, untangling herself from the covers. "No turning the radio on until I get back."

Kim cupped her hand and swatted Chase's ass as she hurried into the bathroom. She managed to shove the door almost closed. She could make out Chase's reply.

"Depends on distraction tactics when you get back," Chase shot back.

Kim dried herself. Slowly flushed the toilet, watching the commode empty and water begin rising. The pipes groaned and pinged. Like possibly three hearts had in the past. Were the powers that be signaling them that their hearts were still pined for what might have been? Was this a signal they had a second chance?

Kim made her way back to the makeshift bed. She stepped between Chase and Slade and sat down. She pulled the covers over her legs. "Nature's call done. Time to check on the outside world. Time to decide if we stay holed up or begin packing up."

Chase sighed, pulled the radio out from under the stool, and started cranking it. "Even if it's passable out. I vote we stay holed up for a while longer. Not like our businesses can't get along without us. We can text we're okay and taking some time off."

"Can we keep our staff away? Keep Michael and the rest at bay?" Slade tucked his hands behind his head. "Our animals know we need time off."

Kim glanced at Slade and Chase. "You got signals from your other halves. I'm trying to read signs from my totems and nudges from my inner mix."

Crackling and static sounded. WXNP's announcer's voice poured out the radio's speaker.

"WXNP here. Beautiful sunlight. Limited clouds. Storm radar shows storm front cleared out of the area overnight. Before you dash outdoors, listen carefully. Roads are still impassable in many areas. Creeks and drainage ditches are flooded or draining slowly. Local and state officials are asking everyone to stay put for today and possibly tomorrow. If you need food or shelter, call local police dispatch for locations in your area. This is WXNP signing off until next update. Three hours from now. Cauldron Falls and Sylvan Valley time check is eleven a.m."

Chase shut off the radio and placed it back under the stool. He picked up Kim's cellphone. He glanced at the screen. It showed three test messages and a quarter battery charge left. He held out the phone to her. "I say send two texts. One to Michael saying Slade and I are okay. You one to your check in person."

"I'll add. If we need anything, we'll reach out. Limited battery power." Slade grinned, adding, "And everyone stay home or where they sheltered until we check in later on today."

Kim snorted. "We can save battery life by not answering more messages until late afternoon."

"Yup," Chase said, laying the phone in Kim's lap.

"I second," Slade added.

Ten minutes passed while Kim sent the two text messages. She handed her phone back to Chase. Had they taken another step into a deeper internal layer of putting their past fears, current angst, and imaginations to rest?

Slade laid on his back as he spoke. "We're at a point where we move forward or keep looking back. Feet forward is my preference. Past can't be changed. Kim helped Terrence out. Good stuff. He was a great friend to all of us. I still need to know why you didn't come back when Terrence dropped you."

Kim hugged her knees to her. Did she let more of her past out? Explain things that only a few people knew. The tormentor was gone. His blemish on her life pulse had faded over the years. Her counselor said talking about it would continue to defuse it. She clasped Chase and Slade's hands. "There's more to why I eloped. Terrence was helping me."

"It's okay if you don't want to talk about it." Chase squeezed her hand.

Slade sat up, slid his arm around her shoulders, and hugged her. "Sorry for opening up bad memories."

Kim brushed her lips over Slade's. She turned to Chase and kissed him. She let go a long sigh. "The person won't be named. I went through counseling for quite a while. My counselor and I dubbed the person Tormentor. Terrence knew a group of mixed-breed hybrids. They offered Terrence and me a place to belong. Getting away from the Tormentor meant giving me room to find out who I was, what my magic traits were and any animal shifter traits I might have."

"I can name several who might wear that blasted moniker well. They all matured. Chase and I had our packs and clans. We knew who we were from our first shift and full moon run. You were an outcast among most. Sorry, we didn't know." Slade hugged her again and let go.

"Damn, Kim. Teen hormones are bad enough with human puberty. Shifter and magic ones complicate things on their own. You had compounded effects happening." Chase slipped his arm around her waist, hugging her to him.

"That was part of why I ran. The other part was needing acceptance. I didn't find it within my own family much. Aunt LaGina and her business partner, Christine, helped as much as they could. They understood why I left once I let them know where I was and why I wasn't coming back anytime soon." Kim pulled her hands away from Chase and Slade. "I'm sorry I put you through crap. I did what I needed to for me."

"Kim, it's okay. You're here. We're here. I'm glad you shared what you have. I never stopped caring." Chase scooted away from Kim.

Slade pulled his sweatshirt over his head and tossed it toward the foot of the makeshift bed. "Once we told each other that clothes hid us from each other. We stripped down, embracing each other and enjoying the chemistry flowing between us. Are we open to igniting that bond again? Forming a new us alliance that is strong and ready to take a chance on us?"

"A new alliance of what, Slade?" Kim turned slightly, watching Slade intently. "Chase cares. He admits it. I care. He and I are getting a friend bond happening. Your intent, I'm not sure about."

"Wolves show their surrender by exposing their belly. Tucking their tail and exposing their throat. I could shift. That wouldn't help. We're dealing with our human parts." Slade laid his hands palms up on his legs where each of them could see them. "One of the most vulnerable areas for a human is their hands. Their palms and wrists. I'm showing them now. I'll shuck my clothes and bare all if needed."

"Slade, I think Kim is talking about where your motivation is coming from." Chase laid his hand on his chest, over his heart. "Is it coming from here? Or your head or your gonads?"

"Kim, I tried once to tell you how I felt. Words haven't been one of my strengths when it comes to being vulnerable and sharing my feelings." Slade rolled onto his side. "I cared then. I care now. I'll probably always care. I'm scared to say or admit more. I don't want to hurt you or Chase again. Chase and I salvaged our friendship because we learned to trust each other again."

"It took a while. I think we're trusting each other more than when we ran into each other. We agreed to meet to do business together. Tossed together, we trusted each other to keep us safe. We've exposed bits and pieces of ourselves that we haven't seen in a while." Chase laid his hand close to the top of Kim's thigh. "What is your heart and head telling you?"

Kim let go of her knees and stretched her legs out. Chase's hand slid higher. Closer to her crotch and mons. Kim glanced at Slade. His gaze met hers. His palms still up and his chest bare. She took a breath, held it, and gradually exhaled. Hair on the back of her neck wasn't standing up. Her heart wasn't racing. No erratic beats. Even her stomach gurgled and quieted. All signs she trusted at a lower level that her totems and spirit guides signaled if she paid attention.

"My head and heart are saying I wouldn't be here if I didn't trust you both at some level." Kim laid her hand, palm down, on Slade's chest.

"Thank you for trusting me. I still care." Slade put his hand, palm down on Kim's. "I'm adding I want more than friends with benefits. I know it's going to take time to get there."

"Slade and I admitted we're not wham bam thank you ma'am males." Chase slipped his hand under Kim's sweatshirt. "We were sexually compatible once. Could we be again? Be more than like Slade said, friends with benefits?"

Kim licked her lips. Her gut said be careful. Her heart pulsed a steady rhythm of go for it. A message whispered through her mind. *Move forward at your pace. You are able to defend yourself if needed.*

"Here's my ground rules. I say stop, we stop. If you say stop, we stop. It moves as fast or slow as all agree." Kim waited for a sign or response Chase and Slade agreed. She fisted her free hand, ready to punch and curled her fingers on Slade's chest ready to scratch if needed.

Slade moved his and Kim's hands as he sat up. "I agree. I'm adding health discussion upfront. Condoms for intercourse. If we move forward, we're fluid bonding with each other. A closed triadic relationship for now."

Chase kissed Kim's cheek and removed his hand off her stomach. "I'm agreeing with both. My addition is keeping us between us. Not telling others for a while. Too many knew last time and tried to worm their way into doing us their way. We gotta do what works for us."

Kim shucked her sweatpants, socks and one sweatshirt. She turned in a circle as she spoke. "I'm partially baring me. Trust builds on words and actions. I'm risking some action now. Mutual nudity we all agree to. My health statement is disease-free including STDs and natural birth control. Condoms. Last check-up six weeks ago before I took over Owens."

"My turn to bare some." Chase clasped Kim's hand and let go. He tossed his socks and sweatpants off. He pointed to his briefs. "Yeah, lavender is my fave color. My health statement is no STDs either, and disease-free. Last check-up three months ago."

Kim grinned and sat down. "Your turn, Slade."

"Okay, so you all get to ogle my briefs. Stark white and virginal my mother used to call them." Slade pulled off his sweats and snapped the waist of his briefs. "My health statement is similar to both of yours. No STDs, disease free and last check-up two months ago.

Kim nudged Chase. "There's a box we need."

Chase got the box. He placed it in Kim's lap. Kim opened the box and pulled out several condom packets. She handed Chase and Slade two each. "Put them where you know they are. I'm washing up and taking a chance on baring it all when I come back."

Kim pushed the bathroom door closed. If the rustling she heard behind her indicated anything, a couple of naked—no nude was the tantalizing word—men awaited her return. She turned the toilet sink faucet on. Warm water gushed out. She wet one of the damp towels, worked soap into it and washed her face, armpits, mons, and labia. As she rinsed off, she made out two words Chase and Slade said. Oral sex and tasting. Kim shivered. Chase and Slade knew how to bring their partner pleasure multiple times.

Chase and Slade backed away from the bathroom door. Slade grabbed one of the damp kitchen towels and tossed another to Chase. "Good thing we found the bar of soap on back of the sink. Moonlight does illuminate things rather nicely."

Chase undressed, wet, and soaped his cock and balls, rinsed, and dried himself. "When the moonlight illuminates the pheromone and hormonal waves pulsing through the room and over those present, you know you're in the right place. Waiting for those present to signal time to move forward."

Slade finished washing his cock and balls. He used the other end of the towel to dry off. "True, my friend. With humans, words and actions backing each other are their signals. Let's get back under the covers and see where things go from here."

CHAPTER EIGHT

Kim opened the bathroom door. Chase and Slade weren't by the other sink. She sniffed the air. Soap, water, and linen greeted her. This wasn't her cleansing lingering from behind her. It greeted her, softly rippled over her and down across her neck and exposed flesh. Tinges of male hormones wisped past her nose and caressed her libido's external heat wave.

She took two steps forward. Rustling of covers and pheromones rushed toward her. Chase and Slade were back under the covers. Kim continued across the room until the makeshift bed, Chase, Slade, and a bunch of discarded clothes came into view. She inhaled deeply. Chase's light, masculine scent greeted her first. Slade's stronger aroma, plus a slight pine scent mixed together, washed over her next. Each blended and part of each kept their markings present. Her mountain lioness totem purred and mewed. Next to her lioness, the golden and green macaw perched on a palm tree limb watched. Her feminine side, with her polyamory trait, announced their acceptance.

Kim stepped onto the makeshift bed between Chase and Slade. She shoved her panties down over her hips, past her knees and down around her ankles. Chase tipped his head back, smiling and holding out his hand. She took hold of Chase's hand, steadying herself. Slade leaned forward, worked her panties away from her feet and ankles. He tossed them on the pile of clothes at the foot of the bed.

Chase pulled back the covers. "Come join us. Snuggles and cuddles are offered. Nude ones are the best for oxytocin generation and release. Great way to turn each other on, too."

"Help you with your sweatshirt?" Slade slid his palm under the hem of her sweatshirt. Warmth mixed with a bit of chill teased the area between her navel and mons. The area where her desire pooled ready to boil up and ignite other parts of her.

Kim knelt and raised her arms. "Learned joining the party, evening out the status is much more fun than going alone all by yourself."

Chase rose on his knees. Slade did the same on her opposite side. Each worked the sweatshirt sleeves over her hands and wrists, freeing her arms and glimpses of her bare breasts. Chase and Slade stood working the sweatshirt up and over her chest, neck, and head. Chase tossed the sweatshirt over his shoulder. Kim noted where it landed. Not too far from the rest of their shucked clothes.

Slade lay on his side facing her. "Nothing happens unless we're all ready. Go ahead and get comfortable."

Chase sat next to her. "It's warmer under the covers sharing body heat."

Kim nodded and stretched out, easing her feet and part of her legs under the covers. "I'm baring all of me. You are baring each of you. This is a new level. A new beginning to something we build together."

Slade trailed his fingers down and across her mons, tracing the edge of her pubic hair. He cuddled closer. "My reaction is evident."

"Mine, too." Chase nestled closer. His hard-on rubbing against her hip and thigh.

Kim clasped Slade with one hand and Chase with her other. Low groans and brief moans sounded from each. "Threesomes work when everyone is pleasured."

"Or two stir up the heat and get the third very hot and bothered." Chase suckled one of her nipples between his lips, worrying it with his teeth and soothing with his tongue.

"Both doing the same thing increases the pleasure and heat throbbing through everyone." Slade cupped her breast, traced her areola with his tongue, and captured her taut nipple between his lips.

Suckle, nip, and lick shudders awakened pulses of slight pain mixed with endorphins flushing over her down inside and out. Her clitoris swelled, matching the tautness of her nipples. Pleasure shuddered up and down her. Her inner fire reaching volcanic levels.

"Ahh! Much more and I'm gonna..." Kim's vision blurred. Her clitoris pulsed. Her nipples throbbed. Juxtaposition happened with each vibration racing over and through her.

As if he could read her, Chase stroked his fingers down her leg until he reached her mons' apex. First one finger, then another stroked between her labia lips. Kim jerked, rocking her hips forward. Slade copied Chase's movements. Two sets of fingers found her wetness. Slicked them with it and stroked her clitoris in slow and then fast strokes. Kim parted her legs. All she could do was feel and rock. Rock her hips toward the hands stroking over, around and across her clitoris. Much more and—"*Oh Deity, I'm there*!" Kim halted mid rock. One orgasm pulse after another zoomed over and back up as Slade and Chase kept suckling and worrying her nipples and clitoris.

Chase let go of Kim's nipple, slowly moved his hand from between her legs, and sniffed his fingers. Fertility tickled his nostrils and moistened his tongue. Tasting Kim had always been one of his favorite sexual acts. She rocked against his face, rubbing her over him as he suckled and licked her clitoris like he and Slade had her nipples. His intensest pleasure was thrusting into her as she orgasmed from him suckling her nipples and stroking her clit as she rode him. Slade got off on positions and watching others as he thrust in and out of his partner. How did they work this out?

Slade rubbed his hand up and over Kim's thigh until his hand lay on her and him. Kim placed an open condom packet in his hand. His cock ached with need. He reached down with his hand slicked with Kim's orgasmic wetness. He stroked down and up, cupping his fingers around his cock head. His pre-come wetness slicked his hand more. Slade stroked down, working the condom over his cock. He kept glancing at Kim and Chase. Both watched him.

"I'm not going to last much longer. Chase, watching you and Kim is going to rocket my orgasm to tsunami proportions." Slade started stroking faster, cupping his balls to him, and fondling them. "Go on with penetrating her if you both want."

Kim picked up the condom packet closest to her, tore it open and held it out to Chase. Chase guided her hand down and onto his cock. Wetness trailed across the back of her hand as Chase guided her hand lower. Lower to where his hand encircled his cock.

"Put the condom on me. Help me do it, please." Chase lay back, holding himself with both hands. "Ride me like before. Engulf us in the heat of caring and pleasure."

Kim rölled onto her knees. She worked two fingers inside the condom, elongating it. She held Chase close to where his hands were. Steadying him, she worked the condom down and over him. Murmurs and tight-lipped moans greeted her as she pushed Chase's hands lower. Lower her hand and fingers moved, easing the condom over Chase's cock until her hand touched his hand fondling his balls.

"Don't know how long I can last." Chase lay on his back, holding his cock with both hands. "I want to sink deep into your heat. Rock us to mutual release, darlin'."

Kim straddled Chase, gently holding him as she sank down on her knees. He rubbed against her twice. Kim rose a bit, eased forward, guiding Chase home.

"Yes," Slade moaned. "Work her nipples and clitoris. Wanna see you come Kim. Hear you getting off with Chase and together."

Kim reached out toward Slade. His hand clasped hers. Chase's hand slid between her legs, finding her throbbing clitoris. He slicked his fingers with her wetness and started stroking. He rolled her nipple between his fingers as if he were tightening a screw. Pull, tweak, turn, and repeat. She rocked forward. Chase thrust into her and pulled back, almost out of her. He thrust forward again, picking up speed. Countering his tugs and twists rhythm on her nipples.

"Forgot how good this is." Kim tried to pace her rocking to match Chase's. "Multiples. Strong multiples. So-o-o close."

"Yes, come Kim. Come for Chase and me," Slade managed to say. "*I'm there!*" Slade groaned.

"*Right with you*!" Chase moaned. "Kim, let me feel you come with *me*." Kim tightened around him. Squeezing, rippling all around and over him. He tweaked her nipple, rubbed his thumb fast over her swollen clitoris and thrust deep into her. Balls deep inside the one woman who pleasured him like no other. He thought he'd never feel this intense, wonderous mind mind-blowing orgasms again.

Kim tightened again, blasts and bursts of her own strong double orgasm rocked through her. Her clitoris plumped, throbbed, and she felt her own female ejaculate ripple out of her. Her vagina pulsed with its own rhythm pumping forth wetness down out of her coating her internally, ready to receive semen if any were present.

Kim slumped forward, bracing herself on her hands on either side of Chase. She focused on a quick mental prayer that both condoms held. Children were not a surprise she was ready to deal with. Her heart and psyche kept whispering the L word like it was a secretive mantra. She wasn't ready for that. Reconnecting took more than physical chemistry and attraction. Had they gotten that part of the remaining elephant manure cleared out of the way metaphorically and possibly plainly?

"Relax and take your time separating us. I've got a hold of the condom." Chase nipped her neck and whispered, "That was wonderful. Thank you."

Slade stood, covering his cock and balls with his hands. "Going to clean up. Quick wash and rinse. Hope the water ain't too cold."

"I got warm water out of the faucet earlier," Kim called out as Slade passed her.

Chase tipped his head back noting where Slade was. After Slade closed the bathroom door, Chase spoke. "I'm picking up on your uneasiness. If the condom broke, I'm not walking away. We'll handle that together."

"Thanks. Appreciate it." Kim swung one leg between her and Chase. She carefully laid her hands on Chase's chest, balancing herself as she knelt on one knee. "We got obvious stuff out of the way. What about beyond now?"

"Gonna take time. Effort and time. Frank discussions." Chase helped her roll onto her side as he pulled out of her, both hands around his condom covered cock. "We continue talking. All three, present. Make sense?"

"Yes. Copies my thoughts." Kim sat up.

"The water is tepidly warm." Slade stood at the head of the makeshift bed. "What you talking about?"

"All of us talking together. Some things will between two of us. But—" Slade interrupted Kim.

"There's no buts. It's yes and so we move forward. If things aren't working, we regroup. Our friendship and us in whatever form that comes out is precious and priority." Slade helped Kim to her feet and kissed her cheek. "Go wash and rinse. Chase and I will be here."

Chase chuckled. "Ain't going much of anywhere streaking about for sure."

Slade laughed, adding, "I gave that up before it came in vogue and way before it went out of style."

Kim snickered, entered the bathroom, and pushed the door partially closed.

"Dude," Slade began, lying down on his side of the makeshift bed. "I don't need to know what you said to Kim until she's back in the room. Too many unsaid and mispokens happened before."

"Agree with you one hundred percent." Chase stood. "I'm going to get this condom off. Where did you put yours?"

"Wrapped in toilet paper in trash can. Hope yours withstood." Slade pulled the covers over him.

"We'll know shortly." Chase trotted to the bathroom. Kim was toweling off as he entered.

"You okay?" Chase asked, working the condom carefully off him.

"Yes. Water warmed up a bit more. Run water in that to see if we gotta talk about oops, please." Kim hung up her towel.

Chase turned on the faucet, held the condom under the water flow, and watched. Kim's breath warmed his shoulders and neck.

Kim kissed Chase's cheek. "No drips below. No water running out. Only the overflow from filling it."

"Yup. My turn to discard it and wash up." Chase wrapped the condom in toilet paper and tossed it in the trash. "Meet you back at the cuddle zone."

"I'll wait to share the news until Chase is back." Kim sat next to Slade smiling.

"I hope that is a good news smile." Slade pulled Kim into his arms. He brushed his lips over hers and worried her earlobe with his teeth. "Just want to let you know I care and am glad we've rekindled our friendship."

"Thanks," Kim whispered and kissed Slade passionately. "Just practicing, okay?"

"Practicing what?" Chase asked, moving on to his side of the makeshift bed.

"Kissing passionately," Kim offered and faced Chase, her lips puckered.

Chase pressed his lips on hers. Traced her lips with his tongue and pulled back. "Not bad practice session."

"Mine wasn't either," Slade quipped. He yawned twice. "I could nap."

Kim and Chase yawned. "Catchiness happening," Chase managed to get out between two more yawns.

Kim pulled the covers up, smoothing them over her and Chase. "I say nap happening now. We eat when we wake up again."

"Right with you," Slade murmured.

"Cuddling and snuggling nap commences now," Chase muttered.

Kim glanced at Chase and Slade. Her smile deepened. Whatever the future brought. Their trio was building a stronger soldier foundation than their prior one.

Kim roused, cocked her head, and lay very still. Had she been humming Loving the Three of Us by Shapeshifter Blues? Music sounded again. Louder this time. Was someone outside with their car radio playing? Wait, no one would be outside unless. . .the music grew in volume, followed by a loud hum and buzzing. Kim sat up, clutching the covers to her. That was her aunt's designated ringtone. Polyamorous matchmakers for the elite matchups later in life. More choices. Better options. Kim attempted to reach over Chase to grab her phone.

"What?" Chase roused. "Who's phone is ringing?"

"Mine," Kim said, tucking the covers under her arms. "Looks like we been found out. That's my Aunt LaGina's designated ringtone."

Chase handed Kim her phone. Slade sat up, whistling along with the ringtone. Kim motioned for Chase and Slade to zip their lip. She doubted either one would comply.

"Hi, Aunt LaGina. I'm fine." Kim nudged Chase. He covered his mouth and still snickered. Slade pressed his lips together, shaking his head. His shoulders shaking with his repressed mirth.

"You want to know where I am?' Kim fumbled with her phone. She caught it as her aunt's voice rolled out of the speaker. "Yes, I want to know where you are and with who?"

Kim glanced at Chase and Slade. They nodded vigorously. Kim looked down and back up. Chase was reaching for her phone. "Aunt LaGina," Kim began, with Chase and Slade chiming in, 'we're together taking a second chance on us.

EPILOGUE

Four Days Later

A full red hunter moon video loomed on the two large wall-mounted screens at the front of Owen's dining area. Michael and Adam had edited the video forwarded by three of their European family members. Kim stood near the bar watching the gathering crowd. Aunt LaGina and Christine sat under a spotlight center of the dining area dance floor. The line of men and women hoping to make full moon matches was dwindling down. Word of the older folks' Sadie Hawkins Hunter Moon fest drew quite a crowd. Aunt LaGina's old beau, Nathan Moonstone, stood next to her handing out name tags and checking names off each list her aunt handed him. Christine's steady suitor, Brian Calstron, sat next to her grinning and handing out numbered cards. Order and mischief were waiting and swirling. Waiting for the Hunter's Moon magic to ignite the evening's festivities.

Chase leaned against the opposite end of the bar, sipping his soda and admiring the view. Slade sat on the barstool next to him, pointing out potential matchups. Who would win the bet on the most matchups made wouldn't be known until morning, if then. Chase leaned toward Slade. "You got the boxes?"

Slade patted his pants' pocket twice. "Yup. Date and initials inside."

LaGina stood and reached for the microphone. Nathan held up the microphone and spoke. "Ladies and Gents, before we begin tonight's first dance, a couple persons asked for a brief moment. Chase and Slade, the microphone and floor are yours."

Chase and Slade entered the spotlight area. They each held the microphone. "We're going to be brief," Slade began. "Youth brings people together. Life, circumstances, and experiences can separate us. Sometimes you get a second chance."

Chase picked up where Slade left off. "Sometimes you learn that healing happens from the inside out. It's when friends, lovers, and those you choose to call family reunite, you learn what the real meaning of cherish is, seeing love grow, and truly understand second chances happen one chance at a time. Kim, would you join us, please?"

Kim wiped her hands on her skirt. Her aunt and Christine motioned her forward. Kim walked into the spotlight circle illuminating Chase and Slade. Chase went down on one knee, holding out an open box. Slade doing the same beside him. Together they spoke. "Kim, we're asking for a moonlight match. A second chance on us and our triadic love."

Kim knelt, leaned to the microphone, and whispered her reply. "Yes! Here's to us, love and our second chances, one chance at a time."

Don't miss out!

Visit the website below and you can sign up to receive emails whenever Solara Gordon publishes a new book. There's no charge and no obligation.

https://books2read.com/r/B-A-RAUJ-ZGCCJ

BOOKS 2 READ

Connecting independent readers to independent writers.

Did you love *Under A Hunter Moon*? Then you should read *Blue Moon Valentine*[1] by Solara Gordon!

[2]

Returning home is never simple—especially when love, secrets, and unfinished business are involved.

Erick Cauldron thought he'd moved on, but Bianca Sylvan's unexpected appearance at a city planning meeting forces him to face his past. The budget issues are nothing compared to the emotional chaos they've stirred. Their complicated history is a powder keg primed and ready to explode.

Toss in Bianca's teenage twins, the mystery of their father, two matchmaking grandmothers, and an upcoming blue moon Valentine's Day—the chaos is more than just a budget problem—it's personal.

Can Erick and Bianca figure out where their individual missing puzzle pieces fit together, overcome their past and build a future together?

Read more at https://solaragordon.com/.

---

1. https://books2read.com/u/3GOnwn

2. https://books2read.com/u/3GOnwn

Also by Solara Gordon

Cascade Bay
Love Reborn
Reunited By Choice
Love's Triple Play
Three Hearts In Love
For the Love of Three

Cauldron Falls
Believe In Love
Home for the Holidays
Three Hearts Entwined
A Mate of Their Own
Moonlit Match
A Christmas Reunion

Cauldron Falls-Sylvan Valley Founding Families
Blue Moon Valentine
Under A Hunter Moon

Peyton Corners
Falling for You

Caught by Love's Slow Burn

Sylvan Valley

No Other Magic Necessary

Claimed by the Wolf

Standalone

A Heart's Desire

To Love You Again

To Love You Again

Watch for more at https://solaragordon.com/.

About the Author

Solara loves and lives with her partner of 21 years in the Metro DC area. What started out as a bi-coastal romance soon settled on one coast.

A vivid imagination keeps her busy creating her next fascinating romance. She enjoys creating unique characters and watching their journeys unfold. "Love freely given multiplies and will return endlessly" is a key aspect of her stories. Add in alternative lifestyles and her love for the paranormal, and the uncommon becomes the norm in many of her stories.

Her day job in the financial services industry pays the bills while she pens her erotic tales.

Read more at https://solaragordon.com/.

www.ingramcontent.com/pod-product-compliance
Lightning Source LLC
LaVergne TN
LVHW090617110826
845146LV00001B/429

* 9 7 9 8 9 9 5 1 8 3 6 1 7 *